BRADFORD SCOTT

GUNSMOKE
TALK

WILDSIDE PRESS

"We're going to hit!"

Slade's cry warned the others to brace themselves as the train bucked, then seemed to leap in the air, grinding to a halt with the cars angled crazily across the track.

From in front came a booming sound, followed by a crackle of gunfire. Bullets whizzed through the shattered windows.

"It's a holdup!" Sheriff Serby bellowed. He and Slade hurdled the sprawled passengers in the aisle and in an instant were on the ground outside the train—facing half a dozen masked men!

Immediately the concentrated fire of the bandits' guns was turned on Slade—with no shelter from the sizzling lead, the Ranger had only one defense against sure death—*ATTACK!*

GUNSMOKE TALK

1

To THE NORTH RISE the Franklin Mountains, a range of bare, craggy peaks. To the east is an arid area that extends for hundreds of miles, broken by flat desert tablelands—austere, desolate, forbidding, a bewildering contrast to the verdant Middle Valley of the Rio Grande.

To the south and west the mountains again shoulder the valley, the Sierra Madre a drop curtain for Juarez across the river in Mexico. A mile or so west of the Texas-New Mexico Line looms the Sierra de Cristo Rey.

El Paso, the City of the Pass—and such it has been since the *conquistadores* passed that way nearly four centuries ago in their search for fabled treasure—lies directly under the crumbling face of Comanche Peak, spreading out fan-shaped around the foot of the mountain. City of the Mountains might well be a more fitting name for this international town, for on all sides mountains pierce the sky in breathtaking beauty.

Where Ranger Walt Slade, he whom the Mexican *peons* of the Rio Grande river villages named *El Halcon*—The Hawk—sat his tall black horse, suddenly, almost incredibly, the valley bursts on the eye like a vision of paradise viewed from hell's mouth; fair indeed as a Garden of the Lord after the region of deserts and rugged mountains he had traversed.

"Shadow," he said to the horse, "I've a notion that this valley must be what the Garden of Eden looked like to Adam when he glanced back over his shoulder."

Shadow snorted and did not otherwise argue the point.

"But the difference between Adam and us," Slade resumed, "is he was going out, while we are going in. When Adam departed from the garden, he left the snake behind, but from what we've heard there are quite a few of the two-legged descendants of that footless critter in the 'Eden' down there. Which really is a comparison unfair to the snakes, who don't bother anybody so long as they are left alone."

It was not the first time Walt Slade had viewed this

marvelous transition, but for him it never lost its charm, although it did evoke memories of violence and death so out of keeping with the peaceful scene.

Comedies do not necessarily require a wide stage, nor tragedies an amphitheater, for their enactment. And ruthlessness and greed do not necessarily reflect their surroundings. The wastelands to the east would have seemed more fitting for dark deeds and the callous disregard for suffering and the sanctity of human life, but wherever men gather together is fertile ground for lawlessness and strife.

Which was why Captain Jim McNelty, the famous Commander of the Border Battalion of the Texas Rangers, dispatched his lieutenant and ace man to El Paso and the Middle Valley in answer to pleas from local law enforcement officers for help in remedying a situation with which they frankly admitted they were unable to cope.

From the elevation where Slade sat his horse, the wide reaches of the valley were spread before his eyes like a map, until they faded into the blue mystery of the horizon. Here to the east they were lonely and apparently devoid of human life—grasslands upon which grew mesquite thickets, trees and other clumps of chaparral growth.

To the west, beyond that retreating blue line of the horizon, the trail Slade rode would run past farms and orchards and vineyards, but here the empty loneliness was relieved only by occasional clumps of peacefully grazing cattle. Here, to all appearances, was a no man's land, as devoid of human tenancy as when the dawn light of Creation glowed upon it.

No, it was not the first time Walt Slade viewed the terrain, its wild beauty in its surroundings of weird austerity. He rolled a cigarette with the slim fingers of his left hand and sat smoking and drinking in the panorama spread before his eyes.

Slade made a striking picture sitting his magnificent black horse on the crest of the rise, the late afternoon sunshine etching every line and detail. He was tall, more than six feet; the breadth of his shoulders and the depth of his chest, slimming down to a sinewy waist, matched his height. A rather wide mouth, grin-quirked at the corners, relieved somewhat the tinge of fierceness evinced by the prominent, high-bridged nose above and the powerful jaw and chin beneath. His cheeks were lean, deeply bronzed, his forehead broad. His pushed-back "J.B." revealed crisp, thick black hair.

The sternly handsome countenance was dominated by

long, black-lashed eyes of a very pale gray—cold, reckless eyes that nevertheless always seemed to have little devils of laughter lurking in their clear depths.

His dress was that of the rangeland, homely and efficient, worn with careless grace. A critical observer might well conclude that chain mail or evening dress would be worn with that same careless grace of the man who does not wear clothes that are becoming but "becomes" what he may don.

So bibless overalls, soft blue shirt with vivid neckerchief at the throat, well-scuffed half-boots of softly tanned leather and the broad-brimmed rain-shed appeared eminently fitting to the moment and the mood.

Clasping his lean waist were double cartridge belts. From these carefully worked and oiled cut-out holsters protruded the plain black butts of heavy guns. And from those protruding gun butts his slim, powerful hands seemed never far away.

Carefully pinching out his cigarette and casting it aside, Slade addressed the tall black horse with his glorious rippling mane and eyes full of fire and intelligence—

"Guess we might as well be ambling, Shadow; can't spend all day loafing up here and admiring the scenery. About time we both put on the nosebag, too. Long time since breakfast, and not much of a breakfast, either. Maybe somebody can spare a handout for ornery El Halcon and his ornery cayuse."

El Halcon! "The good, the just, the compassionate, the friend of the lowly!" said the Mexican *peons.*

El Halcon! "A blasted owlhoot too smart to get caught!" vowed quite a few folks who didn't know the truth.

"Anyhow—blast it!—no matter what he is or what he ain't, he's the singingest man in the whole dadblamed Southwest, with the fastest gunhand. You take it from there!"

With Shadow traveling at a fast pace, Slade rode down the long slope to the valley floor and continued on his way. He had covered perhaps ten miles of steady going when he reached a point where the trail curved through a bristle of tall and thick brush that extended for some distance. Shadow ambled on, his master lounging comfortably in the hull, his thoughts elsewhere so far as time and place were concerned.

He was jerked back to the present and his immediate surroundings by a sound unexpected and alien to the peaceful hush of the dying day—the hard, metallic clang of a rifle shot. It was followed by two more, evenly spaced.

"Now what the devil!" he wondered. Shadow snorted and pricked his ears. Slade listened intently for more shots. He heard none, but he heard something else that steadily loudened, a low drumming of fast hoofs beating the dusty surface of the trail.

"Sounds like some gent is in a hurry," he muttered. He crowded Shadow close against the encroaching growth, which here was a mite thinner than ordinary. Best to give the unseen rider plenty of room, especially after that ominous burst of gunfire.

Louder and louder grew the hammering hoofs. Another moment and a foaming sorrel horse bulged around the bend and into sight. His rider lurched and swayed in the saddle, seemingly barely able to maintain his seat on the hull. And in a wavering hand he held a gun!

2

SLADE WENT sideways in his saddle as the muzzle of the gun jutted in his direction. It spurted smoke. The slug fanned his face. The sorrel shot past like a streak of goose grease. Slade swore a wrathful oath and reached for the butt of his Winchester snugged in the saddle boot under his thigh. Then he desisted, glaring at the lurching, reeling horseman as he careened around another bend and out of sight. Looked very much like he was wounded and had perhaps almost unseeingly thrown down on something he thought might block his headlong flight.

Also, to El Halcon's keen ears came a second drumming of hoofs, more than one set, coming fast. It began to look like the nervous-trigger gentleman might be the object of a chase. Slade tensed for possible action. It quickly proved more than possible.

Around the bend swooped three more riders. The foremost gave a yelp of alarm, and they jerked their mounts to a slithering halt.

This time Slade went clear out of the saddle. As he hit the ground, a slug yelled through the space his body had occupied an instant before. Another kicked dirt into the air scant inches from his head.

Prone on the ground, Slade drew and shot with both hands. There was a yell of pain, and one of the riders dropped his gun and clutched at a blood-spouting arm. Another yell and the leg of a second flopped wildly out of the stirrup. Screeching curses, the trio whirled their horses and streaked back the way they had come. Slade lined sights with the third man's back, then held his fire. The whole affair had been so absolutely loco as to defy explanation, and he did not wish to kill anybody unless he was forced to. He got to his feet, listened a moment to the hoofbeats dimming into the distance and dusted himself off, growling angrily to Shadow, who, knowing just what to do when lead started whistling, had leaped sideways into the brush.

"Okay, feller," his master concluded, "you can come out. I don't think there'll be a second encore. What in blazes have we horned into?"

If Shadow knew, he didn't admit it and satisfied himself with a derisive snort. Slade mounted, hesitated a moment. He would have liked to trail after the trio, but there was the first rider to consider. Little doubt but that he had stopped lead. Might be badly hurt and in need of assistance. Had looked like he would fall from his mount at any moment.

Turning Shadow, Slade rode back the way he had come. He rode warily, alert for anything else untoward, but the back trail remained peaceful. Finally he reached a point where he could see ahead for considerably more than a mile. The lone horseman was nowhere in sight.

Halting Shadow, Slade rolled a cigarette, lounged comfortably in the hull and considered the situation. Even at the rate he was traveling, the fellow would not have had time to reach the next bend in the trail. So he must have turned off somewhere into the brush. Appeared he was not so badly hurt, after all, and had no doubt gotten in the clear. Of course, he might be holed up somewhere awaiting his pursuers, but Slade thought that unlikely, and he had no intention of trying to find out; he'd heard enough blue whistlers singing songs to him for one day.

"Well, horse," he remarked, "looks like Captain Jim was right, per usual, when he 'lowed there was a bunch of horned toads, raising the devil hereabouts and twisting his tail. That is, if today is a fair sample of the goings on. Yep, looks like we should be able to do a little business in the section, if we manage to stay in one piece long enough. Oh, well, needs must when the devil drives, as the saying goes, so let's amble on our way if we hope to make Clint by not too far after dark. Should be hitting the cultivated lands before long; may learn something from somebody there. That is, if that ruckus had its inception that far northwest. We'll just go and see."

Shadow offered no objection, doubtless reflecting that oats were to be had at Clint to pleasingly supplement the strictly grass diet he'd been on for the past few days, and ambled on at a fairly fast pace.

Slade glanced at the westering sun. Only about a dozen miles to Clint, a shady town of adobe houses and folks who as a rule were peaceful and law-abiding. So much so, in fact, that the community was able to dispense with the services of a town marshal, relying on Trevis Serby, Sheriff of El Paso County, for any required law enforcement, abetted by

Tomas Cardena, the plump and genial mayor whom Slade knew well.

That is, it used to be like that, but if the day's happenings were a sample of present conditions in the section, even Clint might be pawin' sand a mite. Be that as it may, there was opportunity at Clint to put on the nosebag and sleep in a comfortable bed, both of which had their attractions for a healthy young man who had been subsisting on scant rations of late and using the sky for a blanket.

A few more miles of steady going and they reached the beginning of the cultivated lands. Now the trail led between small farms, orchards and vineyards—a scene of pastoral peace and prosperity.

Workers in the fields raised their heads to gaze at the tall horseman, but nobody spoke to him. Slade gradually developed the conviction that he was undergoing a critical appraisal. Also, sensitive to expressions and gestures, he sensed an atmosphere of distinct hostility. Not necessarily directed at him personally, but toward what he might possibly represent. Quite different from what he had encountered when he last rode this way, a couple of years back. Began to look like any stranger was an object of suspicion.

Of course the section might have experienced considerable change in two years. It had always been subject to change. Time was when the population of the valley was almost wholly Mexican, but the steady flow of immigration from the east had changed that. Now Americans, especially Texas-Americans, were in the majority.

Even in comparatively recent years the section had known plenty of turbulence. At San Elizario, only three miles to the left of Clint, Judge Charles Howard, John McBride and John Atkinson, members of the very small American colony at the time, were shot to death before an adobe wall in the final tragedy of the famous Salt War.

Through the brush country, Slade had ridden very much on the alert, carefully studying the movements of birds on the wing and little animals in the growth, against a possible attempted drygulching by the trio of gunslingers, although he thought such an attempt unlikely. Two of the hellions were probably not feeling very good at the moment and had no doubt headed for some place where they could get patched up, possibly Clint.

Now, however, in the region of cultivation, he relaxed somewhat; it was not a good terrain for an ambush.

Sunset flamed in a riot of color that drenched the western

peaks with gold and rose and amethyst and mauve. The mighty shoulders of the Franklins were swatched in royal purple. The towering crest of Sierra de Cristo Rey was ringed with saffron fires. Comanche Peak glowed crimson and violet. Gradually the dusk sifted its blue film of beauty over the farm lands. The bonfire stars of Texas blazed overhead, and it was night.

Slade rode on. Shadow quickened his pace in anticipation of something with which to line his empty belly. And soon the lights of Clint sparkled in the decreasing distance.

Mayor Tomas Cardena, whose duties as Clint's chief executive were not onerous, owned a hospitable cantina which was frequented not only by the townspeople but by sprightly young *vaqueros* from south of the Rio Grande, bronzed and bearded farmers and grape growers, and quite a sprinkling of Texas cowhands. With now and then gentlemen who looked to be punchers but who had not recently known the feel of rope or branding iron. For Clint was in the nature of a "passing through" town and at times frequented by those who preferred to do most of their riding during the hours between sunset and dawn.

At the hitchrack in front of the cantina Slade drew rein. He tied Shadow securely to the evening breeze and entered. Cardena, plump, jovial and efficient, spotted him at once and gave vent to a joyous exclamation. He hurried forward, hand extended, his rubicund features wreathed in smiles.

"*Capitan!*" he exclaimed. "You have returned!"

"Looks sorta that way," Slade admitted, returning the other's grip.

"Ha! This is a day!" chortled Cardena. "We will celebrate with the dinner beyond compare, and the wine of the best. Come, *Capitan!*"

"First," Slade replied, "I want to care for my horse. Chances are you'll remember him, too."

"The beautiful *caballo*, how could I forget?" returned the mayor. "We will take him to my barn at once. Come, I will accompany you."

Outside, Cardena made much of Shadow, who evidently remembered him. Then he led the way to his commodious stable.

"The best," he ordered the old keeper, who also remembered both Slade and the horse. After which they returned to the cantina. Having seated his honored guest, Cardena hurried to the kitchen to give instructions for the preparing of the meal. He returned to the table and occupied a chair, his black eyes twinkling.

Slade liked Tomas Cardena, who was an excellent example of Mexican courtliness and Texas vigor, a combination hard to beat. He spoke both English and Spanish fluently, and in moments of excitement or when he wished to swear with unusual vigor, he resorted to both languages, with an occasional pungent Yaqui expletive thrown in for good measure. Also, there was plenty of stringy muscle beneath his plump-appearing exterior, and he was capable of keeping order in his establishment if the going should happen to get a mite rough.

His cantina, although not overly large, was excellently appointed and softly lighted without being gloomy.

After a while the dinner arrived, and it was all the host had promised for it. He and Slade enjoyed it to the full, for Cardena had not yet dined and El Halcon had been eating sketchily for some days.

The wine, poured with ceremony commensurate to the occasion, was a product of the valley's golden grapes, and Slade considered it the peer of the best France could boast.

"And now," said Cardena, after the dishes had been cleared away and they were left alone over coffee and cigarettes, "and now, *Capitan*, what brings you here?"

"Trouble," Slade replied, "or so I have been given to understand."

"Aye," nodded Cardena, "there is trouble here."

"Just what is the trouble, Tomas?" Slade asked.

"The trouble," Cardena replied sententiously, "is the Starlight Riders."

"Starlight Riders," Slade repeated. "Quite poetic."

"Yes," Cardena agreed grimly, "very poetic. It was given them by some loco hombre because they commit their depredations chiefly under the stars. There is nothing poetic about those devils. Not that they aren't artists—with rifle and six-gun. They exact tribute from the farmers and grape growers of the valley, and from the small ranch owners to the east. Those who do not pay suffer."

"Extortion through fear," Slade observed. "It has happened in other parts of Texas."

Cardena nodded. "Back in the old days," he said, *"bandidos* from the south preyed on the valley dwellers in similar fashion. And the attempt to collect a 'tax' on each bushel of salt taken from the Salt Lakes by Mexican carters resulted in the Salt War, in the course of which men died.

"And here," he added, his face hardening, "men have also died."

"So I have heard," Slade remarked. "And have shopkeepers and cantina owners here and in El Paso been approached?"

"So far, not here," Cardena replied. "But I have heard that some cantina owners in El Paso and in Juarez across the river have been approached."

Slade nodded thoughtfully. "Something of like nature was attempted in San Antonio a few years back," he observed.

"*Si*, and I heard that El Halcon visited San Antonio and strangely those practices suddenly ceased to be, and that certain *ladrones* also ceased to be," said Cardena.

Slade smiled, but did not otherwise comment. "Just what all has happened here, Tomas?" he asked.

"Workers in the field have been shot at," Cardena answered. "Barns have been burned, and haystacks. One small farmhouse was burned. And the bodies of the two farmers who lived there were found amid the ruins. They had been shot to death. The whisper goes that they refused to pay when approached by an emissary of the Starlight Riders. Because of the fear of reprisals, it is difficult to get anybody to talk."

"An old owlhoot method—rule by terror, get the inhabitants of a section demoralized and afraid to open their mouths," Slade said. "And Sheriff Serby has been unable to do anything about it?"

"So far," Cardena replied. "He has tried. He visited me here a couple of times, and we discussed the matter and tried to gain information, with no success."

Slade's black brows drew together, and he shot a glance at his table companion. If the situation was as bad as the mayor outlined it, he was developing fear for the safety of Tomas Cardena. Not at all impossible that his cooperation with the sheriff had been relayed to the Riders. Cardena didn't scare easily, was impetuous and outspoken. If the wrong pair of ears had overheard his conversations with Serby, he might well be singled out for retaliation.

Abruptly Slade wondered if he'd already had a brush with some of the Starlight Riders. Began to look a little that way. He reviewed the happening on the trail. An undoubtedly wounded man apparently fleeing for his life, with three others in hot pursuit. And he was revising his former opinion that the throwing of lead at himself might have been but the reaction of nervous trigger fingers. More likely it had been a deliberate attempt to eliminate a witness to a crime or to remove a possible obstacle from their path.

Well, if so, he had taken the first trick, which developed a feeling of satisfaction. He decided to acquaint Cardena with the incident and proceeded to do so.

"What do you think?" he concluded.

"I think," Cardena replied slowly, "that those three men were members of the bunch, and that the one fleeing from them was somebody who had defied them. And they headed in this direction?"

"Apparently so," Slade answered. "I've a notion they were in need of a little medical attention. Would hardly show up in town until after dark, I imagine."

Cardena thought a moment. "Tell you what," he suggested. "Suppose we amble over to the doctor's office and see if he's treated anybody for gunshot wounds tonight."

"Not a bad idea," Slade agreed. Cardena said a few words to his head bartender and they left the cantina.

"Just a short walk," said the mayor. "Reckon you can make it without your horse. Oh, I know—you cowhands, or former cowhands, can usually just make it to the nearest saloon, on foot."

"You malign us," Slade protested. "Sometimes we'll pass up the first one and walk all the way to a second."

"Uh-huh, if it happens to be next door and looks more quiet and peaceful," was the sarcastic rejoinder. Slade chuckled and did not pursue the argument.

It was really but a short jaunt to the doctor's office, and Slade made it despite his high heels, without suffering crippling results. Cardena gestured to a lighted window.

"Doc's up and in his office," he said. "We don't need to knock."

Slade, slightly in front, pushed open the door, and they came face to face with a remarkable tableau.

A man was just gingerly rolling his overalls down over a bandaged leg. The white-haired doctor was applying a bandage to the arm of another man.

Nothing unusual for a doctor's office, but—

Both men wore black masks, and the one the doctor was ministering to held a gun in his hand!

3

SLADE HURLED Cardena back through the open door and went sideways along the wall in the same lightning ripple of movement. The old doctor hit the floor as the room fairly exploded to a bellow of gunfire.

Back and forth gushed the orange flashes, paled by the lamplight. The smoke clouds rolled and swirled. A gurgling scream knifed through the turmoil. A slug ripped Slade's sleeve. Another burned a red streak along the side of his neck. He staggered, recovered, shot with both hands. Then he lowered his smoking Colts, peered through the fog at the two motionless forms sprawled on the floor and began ejecting the spent shells from his guns and replacing them with fresh cartridges.

Cardena came back through the door, his face white as a sheet. The doctor got creakily to his feet and glowered at them both.

"Why in blazes couldn't you show up a little sooner?" he demanded. "I wasted a whole roll of bandage."

Despite the grisly scene on the office floor, Slade chuckled; the old gent was okay.

"We'll make 'em pay for it from what we find in their pockets," he said. "You all right, Doctor?"

"Bruised my elbow but to heck with that," replied the old fellow, vigorously massaging the injured member. "Come here, you, and let me have a look at your neck."

"Just a scratch," Slade deprecated the injury.

"Shut up! I'm the best judge of that," growled the doctor. "The bullets that sort use might be pizened. Come here!"

Slade obeyed, grinning. The doctor examined the slight crease, from which a few drops of blood were oozing.

"I'll smear some salve on it and it'll be okay," he said, and proceeded to do so.

"There, that'll hold you," he remarked. "You were darn lucky, though. Another inch to the right and you'd be there on the floor with those other blankety-blank-blanks. What you young squirts doing here—something wrong?"

Slade gestured to the bodies. "We came on the chance that you might have treated that pair," he said. "Hardly expected to run into what we did. Suppose you tell us just what happened."

"I was sittin' at my desk when that pair came through the door, one of them hobbling on one foot, the other with his hand inside his shirt," the doctor replied. "Both were holding guns on me and demanded to be patched up. Of course I'd have had to treat 'em, guns or no guns—Hippocratic Oath, you know—but them guns decided me to get busy pronto and ask no questions. Was mighty glad to see you gents amble in. A mean soundin' pair, and their eyes didn't look good glintin' through those holes. Was wondering if they mightn't pay my fee with a gun barrel or a sticker, to keep me quiet till they got in the clear. Had been up to some hellishness, is my guess."

"Good guess," Slade nodded. "Tell you about it later."

The bodies lay face downward. Slade turned them over on their backs.

"Got the one that yelled through the neck," commented the doctor. "Caught the other hellion dead center. Good shooting, son! Mighty good shooting!"

Ripping the masks free revealed rather grubby faces with nothing particularly outstanding about them. Except that the glazed eyes, Slade thought, hinted at better than average intelligence.

Cardena leaned close. "I've seen them both before," he announced. "They were in my place a few nights back. Got to talking with one of the bartenders. Said something about riding for a spread over to the east. He told me they asked him quite a few questions—if the place was doing all right, and so on."

Abruptly he ceased speaking and shot Slade a questioning glance. The Ranger nodded; they were both thinking the same thing—that Cardena might be in for an "approach," or would have been had the two devils stayed alive long enough.

Slade began turning out the dead men's pockets, revealing various odds and ends of no significance and a rather large sum of money.

"Hellions been doing all right by themselves." he remarked. "Never earned that much following a cow's tail." He shoved the dinero to the doctor.

"Help yourself," he invited.

"Reg'lation fee for treating gunshot wounds," the old doctor replied cheerfully, pocketing a couple of bills and shoving the rest back to Slade.

"That should be your divvy, son," he added. "You earned it."

"Sheriff Serby can take charge of it when he shows up," Slade answered, stuffing the bills and coins in one of the pockets.

The doctor snorted disapproval. "My name's Doc Tredway, Joe Tredway," he said. "Don't believe I caught your handle."

Slade supplied it, and they shook hands.

"Tomas, what shall we do with the bodies?" he asked the mayor. "We'll send Serby a wire right away, but there's no sense in them cluttering up Doc's office."

"I'll have them packed to my barn," answered Cardena. "Listen!"

Excited voices were sounding outside, drawing nearer.

"Guess folks heard the shooting and are trying to locate where it came from," he said. "Shall we let them in, Slade?"

"Might as well," the Ranger replied. "They can pack the bodies to the stable, and there's no reason for secrecy about what happened. They were forcing Doctor Tredway to treat them, at gunpoint, and started shooting when we entered. Naturally, I had to shoot back."

"Slight understatement, but it'll pass," chuckled Doc Tredway. He stepped to the still open door.

"All right, you loafers," he shouted. "This way."

Another moment and half a dozen men crowded into the office, with more to follow. They stared, volleyed questions. Mayor Cardena did the answering. Suddenly somebody voiced a remark that struck the gathering of curious to silence—

"Betcha they belonged to the Starlight Riders."

Furtive glances were exchanged, and one or two began edging toward the door. Then abruptly a big fellow stepped up to Slade and stuck out his hand.

"Feller," he said in a deep and growling voice, "put 'er there! My name's Hodges, John Hodges, and I'm here to say you did a raunchin' good chore. And if those two skunks belonged to the blankety-blank Starlight Riders, you did a still better one. Them's my sentiments and I aim to back 'em up. Put 'er there!"

Slade "put 'er there" and supplied his own name. They shook hands vigorously.

"Thank you, Mr. Hodges," he said, and turned the full

force of his pale, cold eyes on the silent gathering.

"Gentlemen," he said, "You cannot stamp out evil by fleeing from it. If you display fear, you strengthen the grip it would appear a criminal organization has on this section. I have good reason to believe that the Starlight Riders, as they are called, plan to move into your town, as it would seem they have already moved into El Paso. If you knuckle under, you will ultimately find yourselves helpless to combat their depredations. But honest men who show a bold front always come out on top, sooner or later. Tell the Starlight Riders to do their damndest and go jump in the Rio Grande. That will give them pause, and I promise you I'll do all in my power to help you fight this thing."

"And that'll be puhlenty!" rumbled Hodges. "What you say, boys, goin' to crawl for that bunch of mangy sidewinders? Or are you goin' to string along with Mr. Slade, here, like I'm going to do?"

Faces were hardening, those who had edged toward the door halted, turned back.

"Men," Cardena put in, "your fathers and grandfathers, and mine, fought the Apaches and Comanches and bandits from south of the River to a standstill and made this valley a decent place to live in. I figure we're not showing much respect to their memory if we don't keep it that way. Who's with us to fight this thing to a finish?"

There was a hearty chorus of assent.

"What you want us to do, Mr. Slade?" a voice called.

"If anybody approaches you and demands a portion of your wages or of the profits of your business, bend a gun barrel over his head and get in touch with me or Sheriff Serby pronto," Slade replied.

"We'll do it," voices declared. "We ain't going to knuckle under to a bunch of hyderphobia skunks. We'll do it."

Cardena grinned and chuckled. "You've got 'em," he whispered to Slade. "They'll follow where you lead, come hell or high water. How in blazes do you do it? They were scared silly a minute ago."

"They just thought they were," Slade answered with a smile. "Now let's dispose of those carcasses so Doc can get to bed."

"Uh-huh, I'd better get a mite of rest while I've got a chance," said Tredway. "With *you* in the section, I figure to be a busy man for a while."

"There are a couple of stretchers in my barn," Cardena

said. "Some of you fetch 'em, and we'll pack the carcasses back to the barn. Tell Pedro, the keeper, I sent you; he'll understand."

The crowd, which was constantly being augmented by new arrivals, filed out to attend to the chore. Slade and Cardena were left alone with the doctor.

Old Doc twinkled his eyes at Slade, cast a questioning glance at Cardena. Slade nodded.

"How's McNelty?" Doc asked. "Haven't seen him in a coon's age."

"He's fine," Slade answered. "Will be glad to hear from you."

"Jim's all right," said the doctor. "And he sure knows how to pick 'em. Sends us El Halcon, the notorious outlaw, to uphold the law. As the British band played at Yorktown when Cornwallis surrendered, 'The World's Upside Down'!"

Slade and Cardena both laughed at the sally. Old Doc chuckled creakily.

"Now what?" he said.

"Everything appears to be under control here, so Tomas and I will head for the railroad telegraph office and send Sheriff Serby a wire," Slade decided. "After that, I'm going to bed."

"You'll sleep at my casa, you've been there before," said Cardena. "Take the room you had last time—first at the head of the stairs. My *criados* will let you in—they never go to bed. Then I'll amble back to the cantina before the barkeeps rob me blind. They won't put anything over on the customers, but they figure I'm fair game. Let's go!"

"See you tomorrow, Doc, and tell you about the run-in I had with that pair, down on the trail," Slade said.

"He knew you right off but didn't let on a mite," Cardena remarked as they left the office.

"Yes, he didn't know for sure how much you knew," Slade replied. "I met him first over in Pecos—he's always on the move. How long has he been here?"

"Four or five months," Cardena replied.

"About time for his feet to get itchy," Slade laughed. "He'll stay so long as things are lively here, though. Thrives on excitement, and he's seen plenty in his seventy-odd years. Fine old fellow, a real square shooter with plenty of sand in his craw."

"Yes, he's all of that," agreed Cardena. "Say, wonder what became of that fellow you believe those hellions wounded?"

"I wish I knew," Slade answered. "Perhaps we'll learn something relative to him, before long, if he managed to survive and get in the clear. I wish, too, that I knew where the third member of the bunch is; he wasn't hurt, so far as I could see."

"If he was in town and heard what happened to the other two, I've a notion he made himself scarce pronto," Cardena predicted. "Chances are about now he's telling a mighty angry yarn about you to some others of the bunch, if they happen to be anywhere around. Well, here's the railroad station. I'll send the wire, and then you head for a session of ear pounding; you look tired. And Pete knows you've had enough excitement for one day to satisfy even you."

4

In a comfortable bed, Slade slept soundly until midmorning, arising much refreshed after the first real night's rest he had enjoyed for some days.

"The *patron*, who still sleeps, ordered that you be not awakened," said the smiling young Mexican who served him an excellent breakfast. "Word by the telegraph came from the sheriff that he would arrive on the noon train and await you in the cantina," he added, pouring Slade more fragrant coffee.

After a leisurely cigarette, Slade repaired to the stable for a word with Shadow, whom he found chipper and looking forward to action.

"Take it easy," his master advised. "Your legs will likely be worn down to stumps before we finish this chore."

The blanketed bodies of the dead outlaws lay peacefully against the far wall, awaiting the arrival of the sheriff.

"And even now, if retribution prevails, their souls taste of the fires of *infierno*," the old keeper observed cheerfully. "*El Dios* is just."

Not liking to interfere with true piety, Slade did not argue the point. He bestowed a final pat on Shadow and headed for Tomas Cardena's cantina.

Fortified with coffee and a cigarette, he settled himself comfortably to while away the time until Sheriff Serby would arrive.

Shortly after the whistle of the noon train blew the sheriff—lean, lanky, with a weatherbeaten face that did not move a muscle, but a keen blue eye that twinkled—strolled in. He shook hands with Slade, occupied a chair and ordered drinks.

"So, still collecting 'em, eh?" he remarked.

"Collecting them?"

"Uh-huh, bodies. When the undertaker heard you were in the section again he went out and bought a brand-new hearse. Said he figured to need it."

"I fear he's too optimistic," Slade smiled.

"I doubt it," said Serby, "he's got a good eye for business. Okay, tell me about it."

Slade told him, starting from his ruckus with the three riders on the trail. Serby listened in silence until the account was finished.

"Looks sorta like the Starlight Riders, all right," he commented when Slade paused.

"Trevis," the Ranger asked, "just what do you know about the Starlight Riders?"

"Not much," the sheriff admitted. "An owlhoot bunch, all right, but headed by somebody with more brains than average. We've had some robberies, and stolen cows. That's nothing out of the ordinary for this end of Texas. But extortion is a new wrinkle in this section, and extortion is just what it is."

"How do they operate?"

"Mighty shrewd. Some fellers will ride up to one of the farmhouses, or to a man working in the fields. They'll tell him it would be a good notion to kick in a few pesos for protection against outlaws working the section. If he refuses, they don't make any threats. Just say okay and ride off. Then a few nights later his barn is afire, or some of his horses shot. Or when he's working in the fields, a coupla slugs whistle past his head, mighty close. Doesn't take much of that sort of thing to scare heck out of the farmers and grape growers, and even some of the small ranchers over to the east."

"Looks like somebody could identify the hellions," Slade remarked.

"Uh-huh, if you could get 'em to talk. You can't. I know darn well a lot of 'em are paying—how many I don't know—but you can't get 'em to admit it; they're scared. As Cardena may have told you, two came to me for help, two grape growers who lived alone. Three nights later their house burned down. Their bodies were found in the ruins."

"Snake-blooded killers of the worst sort," Slade commented. "Well, we'll see."

Regarding the expression in his cold gray eyes, Sheriff Serby felt confident that somebody would "see," and in no pleasant manner.

"I understand some of the small saloon owners in El Paso have been approached," Slade said.

"So I heard, in a roundabout way," replied Serby. "But I can't get anybody to admit it. I do know that in one place down by the river a row started just about closing time and the joint was virtually wrecked. A bartender shot. It was rumored that the owner had been sounding off against the Starlight Riders and saying what he would do to them if they tried to hold him up for protection money. As to that, I can't say for sure, but it sounds sorta reasonable. No, we've never had anything of the kind hereabouts so far as I ever heard. It's got me buffaloed."

"Not here, perhaps," Slade conceded, "but it is not new to the West. Take the Brocius gang over in Arizona, for example. With a tight organization and some political pull, they worked it for quite a while. The ranchers of the section paid for protection, or else. No, in one form or another, it is not new. The Doc Skurlock and the Bowdrie outfits plied the same trade, and some mighty big owners came across to safeguard their stock. Handled expertly, there's more dishonest money in it than an occasional stage or bank robbery provide. Hundreds of farmers, grape growers and small owners in the valley and over to the east. With each paying, the take could be mighty big."

"No argument there," agreed Serby.

Slade was silent for a few moments, then he asked, "Any notion where their headquarters is?"

"I've a notion," Serby replied, "that it might be in El Paso. Can't say for sure. We've got a pretty good-sized town, you know, with comings and goings and new faces showing all the time. The hellions could squat right under my nose, and I wouldn't know it. Chances are they have a hole-up somewhere in the hills, too, but I got a hunch that whoever directs operations hangs out in El Paso most of the time."

"Logical to agree you're right," Slade conceded.

"I think I'll have a bite to eat, and then we'll give those carcasses a once-over," Serby said.

"A good notion," Slade agreed. He smoked and sipped coffee while the sheriff put away a hefty surrounding. Then they repaired to the stable.

Serby's examination of the bodies was productive of no results. He could not recall ever seeing them in life. Which, however, Slade did not consider remarkable. He repeated Cardena's opinion that the unsavory pair had visited his cantina.

"Looks like the devils might aim to branch out a bit," the sheriff 'lowed, with which Slade was in agreement.

Motioning the stablekeeper to cover the bodies, Serby glanced at his watch.

"There's a passenger-and-freight due here from the east

at about five-thirty," he announced. "I think I'll have them loaded on that for El Paso. Suppose the coroner will want to hold an inquest tomorrow. You and Cardena had oughta be there; if you can make it."

Slade arrived at a sudden decision. "Tell you what," he said, "perhaps you can arrange to have a stall car hooked onto that rattler to accommodate my horse. If you can, I'll ride with you on the train. Imagine Cardena will go along, too."

"I figure I can do it," replied Serby. "I'll wire Alpine, and I expect they can arrange for a stock car at Van Horn. I know the division superintendent at Alpine. Yep, I've a notion I can do it. Let's head for the railroad station."

With the aid of a couple of messages back and forth, the arrangements were completed. After which they returned to the cantina to consult with Cardena, who had just arrived on the job.

"Sure I'll go along," the mayor said. "Wouldn't mind having a night in the big town. Anyhow, it's big when compared to Clint. Five-thirty, you say? I'll line things up here and be ready. Sit down and take it easy for a while; I'll send over drinks."

"They don't come any better'n Tomas," said Serby. "A plumb gentleman and a fine judge of wine and whiskey."

"Of coffee, too," added Slade, taking a sip.

The combination train arrived on time. Shadow, who was an old hand at rail travel, did not object to being loaded into the stall car and provided with a helping of oats. Slade, Cardena and the sheriff took seats in the coach behind the express car, which was next to the engire. The bell rang, the exhaust boomed and the train headed for El Paso. The three companions smoked and talked. The combination was not noted for speed and would take nearly an hour to complete the twenty-odd mile run to El Paso.

Sunset was not far off when they passed through Ysleta with a dozen more miles to go, and the shadows were growing long. The locomotive chugged along blithely, picking up a bit of speed.

Suddenly the booming exhaust snapped off. Brake shoes screeched wildly against the wheels. The coach bucked and jumped.

"Hang on!" Slade shouted. "We're going to hit something!" He gripped the back of the seat in front with all his strength and braced himself.

There was a prodigious crash. The coach leaped in the air,

came down with its front wheels off the iron, teetered crazily and came to a grinding halt. The express car was slewed around at a thirty-degree angle.

The coach resounded with the screams of injured and frightened passengers who had been spewed into the aisle Thanks to Slade's instant grasp of the situation, he and his companions, although badly jolted, remained erect in their seats.

From in front came a squall of steam escaping from broken pipes. The air quivered to a sudden boom which was followed by a crackle of gunfire. Bullets whizzed through the shattered windows.

"It's a holdup!" bellowed Serby.

5

SLADE LEAPED into the aisle, hurdling the passengers sprawled on the floor, Serby and Cardena floundering after him. He reached the door and whisked out onto the open vestibule. A slug fanned his face.

The next instant he was on the ground, both guns blazing. Yells and curses and a scream of pain arose from the more than half-dozen masked men who had streamed from the brush flanking the right of way. Bullets stormed about Slade. He fired again and again, saw a man fall, a second, a third reel, flounder and slump to the ground.

Now Sheriff Serby was in action. A fourth raider fell. The three who remained on their feet whirled and streaked back into the brush. Slade's gun hammers clicked on empty shells.

Reloading as he ran, he sped down the low embankment and raced to the brush, but as he reached it he heard a clatter of hoofs drumming away. By the time he had forced his way through the chaparral, the three wreckers had disappeared from sight.

"The blankety-blanks!" raved the sheriff, who was crowding behind him. "I wonder if they killed anybody?"

"May have," Slade answered as he led the way back to the train. "Locomotive's turned over, and I think they threw dynamite against the express car door. We'll see."

A scene of wildest confusion greeted their eyes as they emerged from the brush and met Cardena who, though unarmed, was coming looking for them. Yelling and cursing men were streaming from the coaches. The shrieks of frightened women filled the air, with the bellowing of escaping steam adding to the bedlam.

The locomotive lay on its side. The express car was jammed sideways against the tender. All about were scattered boulders and crossties that had been heaped on the track just beyond the apex of a curve.

Slade hurried anxiously to the overturned engine. His fears for the engine crew were relieved when he saw both engineer and fireman, burned and bleeding, but alive and out of the smoldering cab.

The conductor came loping forward, bleeding from a cut head but able to swear fluently.

"Did you get the rest of the blankety-blanked hellions?" he shouted. "No? Well, anyhow you did a prime job on four of them. *They'll* never wreck another train!"

"How about the express messenger?" Slade asked.

"Knocked out a minute by the explosion, but he's come to and 'pears to be all right," the conductor replied.

Slade examined the injuries suffered by the engineer and fireman and decided they were not serious.

"Lucky we were going rather slow," said the hogger. "If we'd been highballing, it would have been different. As it was, we just got flung about in the cab and not pinned under anything. Come on, Tim," he said to the fireman. "Let's beat out those coals before the cab catches fire."

The injured passengers were really more frightened than hurt, and the more composed were looking after the others.

"Yes, a blessing we were just ambling along," the conductor said. "And feller, the chance you took, jumping right out in front of their guns!" he added admiringly to Slade.

"Was the safest thing to do," the Ranger explained. "Resistance was the last thing they expected, and it threw them off balance."

"Oh, sure, plumb safe and easy!" snorted the con. "I got another name for it. What do you think, Sheriff?" he asked, glancing at Serby's badge.

"Oh, I don't pay it no mind," returned the sheriff. "I'm so used to him doing things like that they don't faze me any more."

Slade deftly changed the subject. "Got a telegraph instrument aboard?" he asked the conductor.

"Yep, there's one in the caboose," that worthy replied. "This combination always packs one."

"Then we'll cut in on the wire and notify El Paso," Slade said. "They can summon the wreck train and run a couple of coaches down here to pick up the passengers. Let's go, I want to make sure my horse is all right. With a dozen freight cars absorbing the shock, I imagine he only got shook up a mite, but I want to make sure. Besides, I'll have to unload him and ride the rest of the way to town. You've got your flags out, of course? Don't want another train smashing into this mess."

"Both shacks, front and rear, are on the job," replied the

conductor. "They weren't hurt and highballed into position as soon as they got their brains unscrambled."

Confident that the front and rear brakemen would properly care for their chores, Slade led the way to the rear on the train. Shadow's stall car was the last of the cars behind the passenger coaches and next to the caboose. His disgusted snort relieved Slade's fears for him. A swift examination discovered no injury.

"Take care of you in a minute," Slade promised. He descended from the car to find the conductor with the telegraph instrument and its trailing wires in his hands and dubiously eyeing the tall pole that supported the overhead wires.

"Think you can make it up?" he asked. "I sure couldn't."

"I'll make it," Slade answered. "Can you operate the key?" If you can't, I can."

"I can click out enough to tell them what to do," replied the conductor.

Slade fastened the wires to his belt and went up the pole hand over hand, the conductor watching and shaking his head in admiration.

"Just like a squirrel," he remarked to a couple of passengers who had tagged along after them. "Wonder if there's anything he can't do just right? And I wonder who the devil and what the devil he is? Took charge of things right off; even the sheriff did just what he told him to do."

One of the passengers, a slab-mouthed individual with a leer in his eye, looked knowing. "There are folks who'll tell you he's an outlaw," he said. "That's El Halcon, that folks say is just too smart to get caught. Got killings to his credit. Will get his comeuppance some day."

The conductor glared and tightened his grip on the instrument. "If I didn't need this thing bad right now, I'd bust it over your blankety-blank head, you blankety-blank gossip-spreadin' old woman!" he roared.

"Hey, I didn't mean anything," protested the alarmed passenger, backing away. "I was just telling you what folks say. I don't know whether it's true or not."

"Then keep your blankety-blank trap shut till you know what you're talking about," growled the conductor. "Get outa my way, I got work to do. Killings to his credit, eh? Uh-huh, just the sort as he got to his credit today. Get out of my way, I said."

Perched on the crossarm atop the pole, Slade deftly secured the wires to cut in on the line.

"All set to go," he called to the conductor, who at once began to operate the sending key, rather raggedly.

"Okay," he called back, closing the key. "I got through and made 'em understand. They'll get things rolling in a hurry."

Slade cast off the wires and slid down the pole.

"Now I'll unload my horse," he said.

The conductor and two passengers assisting, the loading plank was lowered, down which Shadow stalked sedately.

"Sure some critter," the conductor observed admiringly. "Betcha he could get you to town faster than this old rattler."

"Wouldn't come far from it, I imagine, if he was in a hurry," Slade conceded as he cinched the rig into place. "Now let's get back to the head end. I want to have a word with the express messenger."

When they arrived at the scene of the wreck, Slade and Sheriff Serby climbed through the shattered express car door to find the messenger sitting in a chair smoking a cigarette and profanely expressing his opinion of things in general.

"Son," the sheriff asked, "just what were they after?"

The messenger hesitated, glanced inquiringly at Slade.

"Go ahead," urged the sheriff. "If it wasn't for him, the chances are right now you'd either be dead or pistol-whipped within an inch of your life; they'd have made you open that safe."

"Not supposed to talk about it," said the messenger, lowering his voice. "Supposed to be a closely guarded secret, as they say. They figured nobody would suspect it being sent by this jerkwater. Better'n fifty thousand pesos in that old box. Closely guarded secret, my foot!"

Slade nodded thoughtfully. He'd had experience with "closely guarded" secrets of a similar nature. Looked like the Starlight Riders had sources of information not accorded to the general public.

"Feeling all right?" he asked.

"Sure," the messenger replied. "Lucky for me I was back away from the door when they flung that stick of dynamite against it. Thought for a minute the sky had caved in."

"Now for a look at those bodies," Slade said as they descended from the car.

Serby had allowed no one to approach the bodies. The masks were stripped off, revealing hard-case countenances contorted in the agony of death swift and sharp, with nothing particularly outstanding about them.

"The sort that's been passing through town all the time

ever since the railroad came and the big boom started," said Serby. "No, I don't rec'lect seeing any of them. Chances are I wouldn't have noticed them if I did—just like a hundred others."

"Suppose we let the passengers have a look," Slade suggested. "One of them might remember something."

But as man after man filed past, peered at the faces and shook their heads, it appeared that nobody could recall seeing the unsavory quartet before. Or if they did, they wouldn't admit it.

"Same old story," growled the sheriff. "You can't get anybody to talk."

And then, unexpectedly, they hit paydirt. The slab-mouthed passenger who had identified Slade as El Halcon paused, peering close by at the dead faces. He looked up, and his eyes met Slade's squarely.

"Feller," he said, "I reckon I made a mistake by sounding off like I did back there by the caboose—seems I'm always talking out of turn—and I'm sorry. And *I* rec'lect seeing two of those skunks, the little one with the speckled face and the lanky one with the red hair. Sheriff, you remember that saloon down by the river that was made hash of a while back? Well, I was in there that night, and so was that pair. I noticed them 'cause them and four or five more were sitting at a table and looking like they were waiting for something—kept looking at the clock. I got a sorta funny feeling and decided I'd better get out of there. Mighty glad next day that I did, when I heard about what happened there. Yep, I saw 'em there. Maybe I talk too darn much, but I don't take up for that sort. Maybe what I just told you might help."

"I've a notion it might, and thank you," Slade said. He held out his hand, which the other took rather diffidently, then hurried off, looking very pleased.

Slade smiled at the conductor, who had joined them. "Never can tell," he observed meaningly.

"Guess that's right," conceded the con.

6

SLADE AND THE SHERIFF began to methodically turn out the pockets of the dead outlaws. Nothing of significance appeared, save a surprisingly large sum of money.

"County treasury is going to get rich," observed Serby. "Hello, what's this?"

He had unearthed a slip of paper on which lines were drawn. He passed it to the Ranger.

Slade instantly recognized the thing as a plat of the railroad between El Paso and Ysleta. At one point a small x was inscribed.

"What is it?" Serby asked.

"Instructions as to just where the holdup was to be attempted," Slade replied. "Fellow who drew it knows his business, too; it's very neat and precise. Also, he is evidently quite familiar with the section," he added reflectively, gazing at the plat with thoughtful eyes.

In fact, Slade was of the opinion that the unknown "artist" had some knowledge of surveying. And anything having to do with a branch of engineering held interest for El Halcon.

Shortly before the death of his father, after financial reverses that entailed the loss of the elder Slade's ranch, young Walt Slade had graduated from a famous college of engineering. His intention had been to take a postgraduate course in special subjects to round out his education and better fit him for the profession he had determined to make his life's work. This, for the time being, was impossible, so when Captain Jim McNelty, with whom Slade had worked some during summer vacations, suggested that he come into the Rangers for a while, where he would have plenty of time to pursue his studies, Slade thought the notion a good one.

Long since he had acquired more from private study than he could have hoped for from the postgrad and was eminently fitted to take up the profession of engineering. But meanwhile Ranger work had gotten a strong hold on him, offering as it did so many opportunities for helping others and advancing the interests of worthwhile people.

In consequence, he was loath to sever connections with the illustrious body of law enforcement officers. Plenty of time to be an engineer; he'd stick with the Rangers a while longer.

A decision which caused stern old Captain McNelty to grin under his mustache.

Often, Slade had found his knowledge of engineering helpful in the performance of his Ranger duties. Right now might well be an example.

"Think it might mean anything?" Sheriff Serby asked as Slade stowed away the paper.

"Can't tell," Slade answered. "Maybe not, but then again it might. I'll study it more carefully later. Well, I guess that's all here, and I'll be ambling. I'll meet you at your office. If they rattle their hocks at El Paso and get that train they promised down here, you're liable to hit town before I do."

"I doubt it," grunted the sheriff. "That cayuse of yours can sift sand when he's of a notion to. Okay, be seeing you."

The trail to El Paso ran not far from the railroad right of way, and when he reached it, Slade sent Shadow northwest at a fast pace.

Slade rode warily, although he did not really expect to encounter trouble. But with conditions what they were in the section, it paid not to take chances. He had covered a little more than half the distance to town when a locomotive shoving two coaches passed him, headed for the scene of the wreck. The railroaders at El Paso had wasted no time.

Doubtless there would be railroad police on the train, who would take care of the express car money. Anyhow, Sheriff Serby would be along to keep an eye on the dinero.

It was well past dark, but he was ahead of the returning train when he sighted the lights of El Paso twinkling in the shadow of Comanche Peak, with the Franklin Mountains looming against the star-strewn expanse of the northern sky. Another half hour and he was tip-tupping through the streets of the town.

Walt Slade liked this boisterous City of the Pass and its sister city, Juarez, built on the banks of that strange, erratic and unpredictable river, the Rio Grande.

Born of the Colorado mountain snows, the Rio Grande flows, a veritable continent-cleaver, for two thousand miles, its moods as varied as the weird contrasts of the land it traverses. A bohemian river, restless, changeful. Today shallow, almost currentless. Tomorrow a raging fury to slash the granite of earth heart. Quiet and peaceful through verdant valleys. Thundering in its sunken gorges. Exacting tribute from the Conejos, the Chama, the Pecos, and Devil River. Till at last, wide and placid, it mingles with the blue waters of the Gulf and is lost in the restless arms of the sea.

And even as its river was the City of the Pass. Ever changeful, ever restless, infinite in its moods, revolting at times but ever alluring. Named for that defile, the iron might of a glacier churned through the mountain wall. El Paso! With a turbulent past, a turbulent present, and a mighty future.

The Apaches had long since ceased making their raids, but their place had been quite adequately filled by prospectors swarming down from the mountains, ably abetted by gunmen and desperadoes who arrived in a steady stream and found the Rio Grande at this point a convenient crossing to and from Mexico.

Things had begun picking up for El Paso when the California gold rush set in. Many of the gold seekers had seen more certain prosperity in the verdant valley than in the problematical gold fields and had stayed their rush to help swell the population. The Civil War and its aftermath helped some, too. But it was the coming of the railroads that really started El Paso on the upgrade. The Southern Pacific, the Texas and Pacific and the Mexican Central from Mexico to Juarez unleashed the flood. Population boomed. The railroad builders passed on, most of them, but in their wake came a rush of Wild West hellraisers, gunslingers and gamblers and their motley following. Gambling halls, saloons, and "other places" blossomed.

Long gone were the days when El Paso was but a huddle of squat, one-story adobes. Now there were plenty of pretentious buildings, and more in the course of construction. That night when Walt Slade rode in from the southeast, El Paso was already quite a town.

Slade turned into East Overland Street and soon reached the courthouse, where he found a deputy occupying the sheriff's office. The deputy remembered him. They shook hands, and Slade briefly recounted the train wreck and the frustrated robbery.

"Trevis should be along any time now," he concluded. "I'll put up my horse and then wait for him here."

There was a livery stable nearby, which Slade had patronized before. There he secured suitable quarters for Shadow, spoke a few words with the stablekeeper, who also remembered him, and, packing along his saddle pouches, headed for a small hotel around the corner, where he signed up for a room in which he deposited his pouches and rifle. After which he returned to the sheriff's office to smoke and talk with the deputy until Serby showed up.

It was a half an hour or so later that the sheriff put in an appearance.

"Everything okay," he said. "I had the bodies packed to the coroner's office. Railroad police took charge of the express car money—it'll go in the express company office safe. Here comes Cardena; he stopped to talk a minute with a feller he knows. Now suppose we go hunt something to eat; I'm feeling a mite lank after all the excitement and everything. You might as well come along, too, Bill," he told the deputy. "Time to shut up shop for the day. We'll go to the place on Texas Street, Walt, if you don't mind. Remember it?"

"Quite well," Slade replied. "It's okay."

As they walked to Texas Street, Slade remarked to the sheriff. "What that passenger told us sort of ties things up a mite. When he said he saw those two hellions in the place you told me was pretty well wrecked in the course of a row. If you are right in your opinion that the bunch that gave it a going over were members of the Starlight Riders, it's logical to believe that the train wreckers were, too."

"Looks sort of that way," Serby agreed.

"Which would tend to show they are branching out a bit, varying their activities to include robbery."

"Right again, I'd say," replied Serby. "Well, they didn't have much luck this time. But," he added somberly, "if we *are* right, it puts you on an even hotter spot than before. They'll sure have a knife whetted from now on."

Slade smiled. "Well," he said, "if I may be allowed to enlarge on your metaphor, we've managed to put six nicks in it so far. That might possibly render them a bit jumpy in addition to hankering for revenge. And jumpy gents are liable to make slips."

"Oh, I suppose so," grunted Serby. "Nothing seems to affect you. I sometimes think you get a real kick out of having a bunch of killers on your trail."

Slade laughed and did not pursue the subject.

"That place that got the going over still in business?" he asked.

"Yep, still doing business, with the damage repaired," the sheriff answered. "One thing you can say for those rumholes down by the river, even if you can't say anything much else, they're paying propositions."

Slade nodded thoughtfully. "Looks sort of like the owner may have knuckled under to the Riders," he commented.

"Could be," Serby conceded. "Well, here we are; let's eat."

Their entrance created something of a stir. Slade quickly noted that several of the combination train's passengers were present, two or three with plastered heads, and with groups of attentive listeners around them. Evidently the wreck and the attempted robbery were under discussion. Admiring glances were cast in his direction. Serby snorted.

"The way those blabbermouths will be telling it, there were a thousand owlhoots and a band of Apaches in on the deal," he said. "You'll be Davy Crockett, Dan Boone, and Bigfoot Wallace all rolled into one. Oh, well, they wouldn't be too far off at that."

"Agreed," said Tomas Cardena. "Let us drink."

They were escorted to a table by the proprietor, followed Cardena's advice and ordered a meal. Sheriff Serby glanced around complacently.

"As I told you before, this is a nice place," he observed. "Hardly ever any trouble here. Maybe we can eat in peace and not have to dodge lead."

"Which has its advantages," Slade admitted. "Listening to blue whistlers can get monotonous."

A big, well-dressed man with an impassive face and keen dark eyes strolled over from the bar.

"Hello, Parker," the sheriff greeted. "Take a load off your feet and have a snort and something to eat. Walt, this is Mr. Bruce Parker. Bruce, I want you to know Walt Slade, an *amigo* of mine and a right hombre."

"It's a pleasure to know you, Mr. Slade," Parker said as he shook hands with a firm grip, his eyes narrowing the merest trifle, which Slade noted. He had a feeling that Parker had quite likely recognized him as El Halcon and did not approve. "I heard about what happened this afternoon. You did a good chore, a mighty good chore.

"Plan to locate here?" he asked as he drew up a chair. "I hope so; we can use men like you."

"Thank you, Mr. Parker," the Ranger replied. "It depends."

Parker looked interested. "If you decide to, drop in at my office on Mills Street," he invited. "I'd like to have a talk with you."

"Thank you," Slade repeated without further committing himself.

"I'll have a drink, Trevis," Parker said. "Then I must be going. Have a busy day ahead of me tomorrow."

He downed the drink, and after a few more words took his departure, glancing back as he passed through the swinging doors.

"Seems to be a purty nice feller," remarked Serby. "Figures to be a promoter. Showed up about six months back and has been buying and selling real estate. Says he aims to build a couple of good hotels here. Says folks are beginning to hear about El Paso and that before long we'll be getting what he calls tourist trade."

"He might well be right," Slade answered.

"Always got an eye out for business," Serby added. "Saw he was looking you over. Smells a prospective customer. I've played cards with him in here a couple of times. Plays a good hand of poker and wins or loses the same. Which you can't say for everybody. Well, here comes the chuck. About time; I'm ga'nt as a gutted snowbird."

A period of busy silence followed, for which Slade was thankful; he desired to do a little quiet thinking.

The subject of his cogitations was the riverfront saloon which the sheriff mentioned, and he determined to pay the place a visit. He purposefully refrained from mentioning his intention, or even asking where the place was located, for he knew perfectly well that if he did so, the old peace officer would insist on accompanying him, and the appearance of the sheriff in the place would instantly tighten latigos on jaws. Whereas his entrance alone would quite likely arouse only momentary interest, and somebody might do some loose talking. Was worth giving a try, anyhow. He knew where he could learn the location of the saloon, which he gathered was not far from the bridgehead.

Sheriff Serby finished his surrounding, took a final swig of coffee and stifled a yawn.

"I'm going to bed," he announced. "Been quite a day, and it's late. Will hold a double-barreled inquest tomorrow. How about you fellers?"

"I'm in favor of it," said Cardena. "How about you, Walt?"

"I'll take you over to the hotel where I'm staying, I'm sure you can get a room there," Slade answered evasively.

Reaching the hotel, Cardena registered for a room, at the door of which he bade Slade goodnight. Slade entered his own room and without lighting the lamp drew a chair to the open window and sat down. Rolling a cigarette, he smoked slowly, listening to the hum of El Paso's busy night life.

After a while he pinched out the butt, slipped quietly from the room and descended the stairs. On the street he sauntered south, gradually leaving the better lighted section of the town behind.

Now he paid careful attention to his surroundings, for this was dangerous ground for the unwary, especially if they looked prosperous. To the casual observer, his stroll would have appeared aimless. However, he knew exactly where he was heading—a cantina near the bridgehead where he was well known and which had always been in the nature of a clearing house for border news. Pablo Montez, the owner, would direct him to the place he sought, and might possibly be able to divulge something relative to the Starlight Riders. Not much went on in the border country that Pablo didn't know something about.

He reached the predominantly Mexican quarter where life moved at an easier pace, where the lighting was softer, the music more soothing. Close to where the bridge across the Rio Grande loomed against the sky he entered Pablo's cantina, where the illumination consisted chiefly of wax candles. The orchestra, a really good one, played muted music.

Heads turned as he entered. Then big, smiling Pablo himself came hurrying to greet him.

"*Capitain!*" he exclaimed. "This is a night to remember! Come to the table here close to the dance floor, where the *senoritas* can look upon one so greatly handsome. Come!"

"When it comes to dishing out really absurd flattery, Pablo, you are in a class by yourself," Slade chuckled as they shook hands.

"Flattery!" Pablo repeated in a scandalized voice. "I deal not in flattery. I speak only what all can see is true."

Slade chuckled again and followed him to the designated table. He refused to admit to himself that the glances of the dance floor girls confirmed Pablo's judgment.

"The wine we will drink," said Pablo. "The wine served only to Pablo himself and to those who appreciate. Be seated, *Capitan*. Waiter! Rattle your hocks, as the *Capitan* would say."

The wine was brought, delectable as to taste and bouquet. Pablo raised his glass and lowered his voice, "To El Halcon, the good, the compassionate, the friend of the lowly. Upon whom *El Dios* smiles."

Walt Slade bowed his head. "Thank you, Pablo," he said simply.

7

THE GLASSES were emptied slowly and in silence, as was fitting to the occasion. Pablo glanced expectantly at his guest as he refilled them with the fragrant wine.

"*El Capitan* seeks something?"

Slade told him what he sought. Pablo nodded his big head.

"*Si*, I know the place," he replied. "It is close, on Stanton Street. It is called the Full-House. It is not of good repute. The owner, one Clay Regan, poses as a hard man, but in the time of stress, as your *vaqueros* would say, his guts turn to fiddle strings."

"So I gather," Slade commented.

"Does *Capitain* seek aught else?" Pablo asked.

Slade broached the subject of the Starlight Riders. Pablo's face hardened, and he replied in the formal and ofttimes poetic English of the Mission-taught—

"Of them, unfortunately, I know not much. Like the shadow that loses itself at sunset and is born again of the moon, they go and they come. They are evil, most evil. They prey on the weak and the helpless. The honest *ladron* who gambles his life to achieve his dubious ends I can abide although I do not approve. But such as those are the spawn of *el Diablo*. This much have I heard, although from sources questionable. He who plans and directs their depredations lurks here in El Paso. I cannot say for sure, but I believe it to be true. Doubtless he hides behind a front of respectability, as did the Pharisee of old."

Slade nodded. "I've a notion you're right," he said. He was glad to have his own deductions confirmed.

"You have not been approached, of course," he stated rather than asked.

Instantly Pablo's eyes were the eyes of the mountain Yaquis whose blood mingled with the Spanish in his veins.

"They approach only those who can be made to fear," he replied quietly. "Pablo cannot be made to fear. Nor can his young men, who are always close at hand."

Slade chuckled. No, Pablo did not fear, and his "young men" were artists with gun and knife.

"Was Regan's place much damaged?" he asked. Pablo shrugged his big shoulders.

"Oh, it was spectacular, as one would say," he replied. "Bottles were swept from the bar and shattered. Chairs were hurled through the air, some broken. Tables were overturned. Some glass knocked out of the windows. A bartender claimed a bullet fired by one of the miscreants grazed his arm. Really, the damage was small, but looked big. Took but a day or two to repair. The place kept right on in business. Perhaps what was done was but a hint of what could be done and perhaps would be done were the owner not receptive to the hint."

"Possibly," Slade conceded, his eyes thoughtful.

"Of course to completely destroy the place would have meant to also destroy its usefulness as a source of gain," Pablo suggested.

"Possibly," Slade repeated, his eyes still thoughtful.

A girl came out of the back room, a rather small girl with great dark eyes, curly dark hair, red lips and a roguish smile.

"You doubtless remember her?" said Pablo. "Carmen, my niece. She has been working on my books, a task I abhor." He beckoned the girl to approach.

"Would be impossible to forget her," Slade replied, rising to his feet and drawing out a chair. There was a glad light in her eyes as she drew near, and she held out a little sun-golden hand over which Slade bowed with courtly grace.

"Be seated, *cara mio*, and partake of wine," invited Pablo. "Me you will pardon, *si*? I must check the bar."

"Obvious, but considerate," laughed Carmen, who was Texas born and spoke Texas English with occasional lapses into Spanish or the stately product of the Mission. "And you have returned, after all."

"How could I refrain?" he replied gallantly.

Carmen laughed again. "Sounds wonderful, but I do not think Carmen was the attraction."

"But she made the opportunity to return very attractive," he answered. "Unfortunately I cannot always order my movements in accordance with my desires."

"Better and better," she said, as he filled her glass. "Almost can I believe it."

"It's true," he protested. "And one thing I promise you, I'm not leaving as quickly as circumstances forced me to last time."

"I hope not," she said softly.

For a while they talked gaily together, as an attractive young man and an attractive young woman will, but when

Pablo strolled back to join them, Slade said, "I'm going out for a while, but I'll be back. Pablo, don't let your *muchachos* follow me."

"You'd be safer if they did," Pablo protested.

"Without a doubt, but with much less chance of accomplishing what I hope to," Slade replied.

Which was true. The presence of Pablo's young men would even more effectually close mouths than would the sheriff's.

"Please be careful," urged Carmen, her beautiful eyes worried.

"I will," Slade promised. "I'm not going looking for trouble, just hope to perhaps gain a little information I urgently desire."

"Yes, but the last time you were here and went out for 'just a little while' you ran into trouble," she reminded him.

"Lightning doesn't strike twice in the same place," he replied laughingly.

"A comfortable superstition, but one that is not borne out by the facts," she retorted. "Please be careful."

After leaving the cantina, Slade took careful note of his surroundings. Everything appeared peaceful, and without mishap he spotted the Full-House from Pablo's description. It fronted on Stanton Street and was backed by a narrow and dark alley which he passed before turning into Stanton.

As he neared the door, a man came out and, glancing about, walked hurriedly down the street without looking around again.

Slade stared after him, for he had recognized him as Bruce Parker, the promoter and real estate man, who had been introduced by Sheriff Serby. What the devil was *he* doing in this rather doubtful neighborhood at well past midnight?

However, he recalled Serby saying that Parker was interested in waterfront real estate, planning to erect one of his hotels close to the river. Which was doubtless the explanation for his presence. Might have been dickering for the location on which the Full-House stood.

Heads turned when he entered, but nobody favored him with more than a passing glance. He found a table, sat down and ordered a drink. The waiter who served him was affable and apparently paid him no mind.

The Full-House was fairly large, rather dingy and not too well lighted. It was fairly well patronized at the moment by a polyglot gathering. There were Mexicans, cowhands, rivermen and others. None of whom gave the impression of being outstandingly sinister, so far as Slade could see. The bar was busy, the dance floor girls weren't too bad, the orchestra quite good. Games at the tables were orderly.

All in all, it seemed to be just an average cheap waterfront saloon, like to quite a few others along the river.

Standing at the far end of the bar, near the till, was a big beefy man whom Slade concluded was Regan, the owner. He studied him as he sipped his drink, his black brows drawing together slightly.

Appearances could be deceptive, of course, but Clay Regan did not look like a man whose guts would turn to fiddle strings when the going got tough. Quite the contrary, in fact.

Pablo had admitted that he knew little concerning the man, who had been called to his attention only after the row in the place and the whispers that the Starlight Riders were responsible. That the opinion he had formed of him was largely based on hearsay. Also, it appeared that the damage inflicted had really been negligible, the accounts of it highly exaggerated. Could have been just an orthodox row over cards or a woman, in the course of which chairs were thrown, tables overturned and a lot of noise kicked up.

There was another angle to contemplate. If the Starlight Riders *had* been responsible, Regan might have acceded to their demands on a business basis, succumbing to what he considered the lesser of two evils. Some big ranch owners in New Mexico and the Panhandle country of Texas had done just that.

Analyzing the known facts, Slade was developing the feeling that what had looked to be a promising lead had petered out. Well, that's the way things sometimes worked.

He ordered another drink and generously tipped the affable waiter, who smiled and bowed.

"Been here long?" Slade asked casually.

The waiter shook his head. "Only a few days," he replied. "Fellow before me quit. Had a bad row with the boss, I understand. Cook told me he wasn't much of a waiter; didn't seem to know anything about the business. Said he used to ride off somewhere and come in late. Liked to ride. Like a cowboy, I guess."

Slade nodded his understanding. Quite probably the fellow was a chuck-line riding cowhand who had taken a stopgap job of waiting on tables to get tobacco and whiskey money. Something not unusual.

The waiter moved away. Slade sipped his drink and continued to study Clay Regan, who somehow interested him.

Suddenly Regan raised his head in an attitude of listening. He turned and walked to a door beyond the end of the bar, opened it just enough to allow his body to slip through and closed it behind him. He did not immediately reappear. Doubtless the door led to a back room where perhaps he had been summoned to check stock or confer with somebody.

After a while Slade concluded there was nothing to be learned in the Full-House. What scraps of conversation he had been able to hear dealt with nothing of significance. He said goodnight to the waiter and walked out.

Turning the corner, he headed for Pablo's cantina. He was nearing the alley mouth when he halted abruptly, staring.

Lying sprawled and motionless on the sidewalk was what appeared to be the body of a man.

Slade took a stride forward, another. He was almost to the alley mouth when he halted again, then hurled himself against the building wall, hands streaking to his guns.

From the alley mouth gushed a lance of flame. A slug fanned Slade's face and thudded into the wall. He shot with both guns, again and again.

A gasping cry echoed the reports. There was a thud, then a patter of swift steps down the alley.

Gun muzzles jutting forward, Slade hesitated an instant, thumbs hooked over the cocked hammers. He glided forward, slowly, until he could peer cautiously into the alley.

The first thing he saw was a pair of feet, the toes pointing skyward. He holstered one gun, reached down and gripped an ankle jerked.

A body slid into view. A single glance at the spreading stain on the drygulcher's shirtfront told him he had caught the hellion dead center. He turned from the outlaw's body and gave the "dead man" on the sidewalk a vigorous kick. The "body" flew through the air and broke in two, scattering straw in every direction, a pair of shoes clattering on the ground, a hat trundling to one side.

Around the corner shouts were sounding. Somewhere up the alley a door banged open. With a single glance at the face of the dead drygulcher, he whirled and raced down the street at top speed, whisked around a corner, another, slowed his pace. He was sauntering when he reached Pablo's cantina.

It had been a nice try, but the devils had failed to count on El Halcon's amazingly keen eyesight and his equally amazing faculty for noting the smallest detail that was out of order and instantly translating its meaning.

Entering the cantina, he glanced about. Carmen was still

at the table where he left her, looking decidedly worried. She exclaimed with relief when he dropped into a chair opposite her. Pablo came hurrying over to join them.

"I thought I heard shooting somewhere," he announced.

"Chances are you did," Slade replied.

Pablo drew up a chair. "Tell us what happened," he urged.

Slade told them, in detail. Carmen's breath caught in her throat. Pablo said things in two languages.

"It was cleverly handled," Slade concluded. "They rigged up the contraption very neatly, even to shoes and a hat. The natural reaction on the part of most anyone would be to hurry forward and bend over the body, or what was supposed to be a body. That's what they expected me to do, of course. I was about ready to do just that when I noticed something that didn't look right."

"Yes?" prompted Pablo, intensely interested.

"Yes," Slade replied. "I never before saw a leg bent forward at a thirty-degree angle at the knee joint. Knee joints just naturally don't bend that way. That's when I went sideways against the building. Fellow in the alley snapped a shot at me and missed, which was a mistake on his part."

Pablo shook his head in profound admiration. "Is there ever anything *El Capitan* does not see?" he marveled.

"Plenty," Slade answered, "but there are some things you just can't miss seeing if you are in your right mind," he added, his eyes laughing at Carmen, who blushed prettily and lowered her dark lashes.

At that moment an excited man rushed in, hurried to the bar and began talking to several others, who leaned close to listen.

"Guess somebody has found the body," Slade hazarded. "We'll be hearing all about it before long. I don't think I was seen leaving the spot, so there should be a lot of wild guessing."

Pablo signaled a waited to bring another bottle of wine.

"I'd like a cup of coffee if you don't mind," Slade said. Pablo gave an order, and the coffee was quickly forthcoming.

"Better for the complexion than wine," Slade remarked. "Guess Carmen must drink a lot of it. Something sure makes the roses bloom in her cheeks."

"It is not the coffee," Carmen flatly contradicted him, and the roses bloomed a little brighter.

Ten minutes later the town marshal, a complacent individual who never seemed much impressed by anything, strolled in. He waved to Pablo and made his way to the table, where he shook hands with Slade before sitting down.

"Busy as usual, eh?" he remarked. "No wonder Serby went to bed early; you wear him out." He turned to Pablo.

"Was told there was a shooting down this way," he said. "I ambled down to see about it. Was over on Stanton Street by an alley. Never saw such a funny killing. Feller, mean-looking cuss, drilled dead center. Another one had all the stuffin' kicked out of him. Must have been part horse and feedin' on hay. Even lost his shoes and his hat. Sure was funny. Wish I knew who did it. Would like to pin a medal on him."

Pablo shook with silent laughter. Slade grinned. And even Carmen, who did not appear in a mood for mirth, smiled wanly. Pablo filled the marshal's glass to the brim. That worthy winked at Slade and quaffed the goblet without taking it from his lips.

"Oughta have a real nice inquest tomorrow," he observed as he rose to go. "Seven prime specimens to set on. See you there, Slade. I wonder how that jigger over by the alley *did* get cashed in."

Pablo glanced at the clock. "It is late," he said. "Carmen, you'd better depart for home."

"I'll walk with you, if I may," Slade offered.

"You may," she replied, her eyes laughing. "I'll get my cloak from the back room."

Pablo glanced toward a table where several dark-faced young Mexicans were sipping wine. They got up and strolled out, one by one. Slade repressed a smile. He knew he would not need to pay much attention to his surroundings when they left the cantina. For until they reached the better lighted and busier section, they would be virtually encompassed by Pablo's watchful and efficient "young men."

Carmen returned from the back room wearing a gay cloak. They said goodnight to Pablo and departed arm in arm. On Kansas Street Carmen paused before a trim little house set in a garden of flowers.

"Pretty," Slade commented.

"Yes, it is," she replied. "Left to me by my dead father. He loved his garden, and I have always kept it just as it was when he lived."

"You live alone?"

She slanted a sideways glance through her lashes and snuggled a little closer.

"Yes," she said softly.

His arm was around her trim waist as they walked to the door together.

8

THE INQUEST held over the collection of bodies was nothing but a formality. Without leaving the box, the coroner's jury rendered a verdict, commending Slade and the sheriff on doing a good chore and 'lowing that the hellion picked up in the alley mouth met his death at the hands of parties unknown but very likely had it coming, too.

Before the bodies were carted off by the undertaker, Slade studied the fellow's dead face.

"I can't say for sure," he told Sheriff Serby, "but I've a notion he was the third member of the bunch chasing that poor devil down the trail south of Clint."

"Wouldn't be surprised," said Serby. "Looks like they're all tieing up with the blasted Starlight Riders, wouldn't you say?"

"It sort of looks that way," Slade conceded.

"Which means you're sure thinning the hellions out," declared Serby.

"Yes, but undoubtedly whoever heads the bunch is still running around loose," Slade pointed out. "And as I've said before, that sort of a head grows a new body mighty fast."

"Guess that's so," the sheriff agreed. "Well, we'll have to try and squash the head. That is, when we know who to squash. What did you think of that rumhole down by the river, where you had to go gallivanting by yourself when I figured you were safe in bed?"

"Frankly, I don't know," Slade replied. "Seems innocuous enough, but you never can tell."

He purposely refrained from mentioning that he saw Bruce Parker, the promoter, leaving the place. To do so would be in the nature of spreading gossip; Parker had a right to go where he pleased in the interests of his business.

Nor did he confide his estimate of the Full-House owner, Clay Regan. For he might well be mistaken in his conclusion, which differed radically from that advanced by the sheriff and Pablo Montez.

"Suppose we go eat," suggested the sheriff. "Inquests always make me hungry. Sorta remind me that it may be quite a while between surroundin's where I'll be going before long. Here comes Cardena. Guess he's ready to eat, too. Says he's going to spend another night in town."

Before the day was over, there was more grist for the inquest mill. A pair of cowhands from one of the spreads south of Clint rode up to the sheriff's office leading a saddled and bridled horse. A body roped to the saddle flopped grotesquely to the animal's movements.

"Found him in the brush the other side of Clint," one of the punchers explained. "Seeing as we were heading for here, we figured we might as well bring him along to you, Sheriff. He's getting sort of ripe. Been dead several days, I figure."

"How did you come onto him?" asked the sheriff, giving Slade, who was in the office at the moment, a swift glance.

"Saw the poor cayuse with a full rig on trying to graze at the edge of the bushes. Saddle was skewed sideways, but he couldn't get the bit out of his mouth. Figured the gent who rode him had oughta be somewhere around close, so we prowled the chaparral a bit and found him where he'd slid outa the hull. Shot to pieces. Maybe you know him?"

The sheriff took a look at the dead face, which was showing signs of disintegration, and shook his head.

"Don't figure to have seen him before," he said. "Not very purty right now. Uh-huh, he's getting ripe, all right. We'll take him to the undertaker's place and put him on exhibition."

This time the exhibition brought results. Rather startling results from the viewpoint of Slade and the sheriff. A riverman dropped in and took a look.

"Say, I've seen this feller before," he announced.

"Where?" the sheriff prompted.

"He used to wait on tables in a place over on Stanton Street," the riverman replied. Slade and the sheriff exchanged glances.

"Remember the name of the place?" the latter asked.

"Sure," said the riverman. "Place called the Full-House. You'll remember it, Sheriff. They had a big fight in there a while back. Remember?"

"Yes, I do," Serby replied. "Feller named Regan owns it, doesn't he?"

"That's right," agreed the other. "He'd oughta remember this feller, even though he don't look exactly like he used to."

"Much obliged," said Serby. "May help us to find his folks, if he left any."

"Guess that's so," nodded the riverman. "Glad to be of help, Sheriff."

He ambled out. Slade turned to Serby. "I think," he said in low tones," that it would be a good idea to send for Regan."

"Right," agreed the sheriff, and immediately dispatched a deputy on the errand.

In short order the saloonkeeper arrived. He took a look at the corpse and nodded.

"Yes, he worked for me," he said. "Wasn't much good as a waiter and had a quarrelsome disposition. Was a chuck-line rider working his way east. Said he came over here from Arizona. Wouldn't be surprised if he had good reasons for leaving Arizona; might have been invited to leave. I finally had to let him go. He kicked up a bit of a fuss, but I cooled him down and got rid of him without any real trouble. Didn't see him after that and figured he'd trailed his twine. Looks like he got into one argument too many."

"Ever hear him mention having any folks we might notify?" Regan shook his head.

"Never mentioned anything much about his past life. Just said he came here from Arizona; sorta gave the impression he was raised over there. That sort usually don't talk much."

The sheriff nodded agreement. "Well, much obliged, Regan," he said. "Guess we'll just have to hold a sorta inquest over the remains and plant him."

Favoring Slade, who had stood silent during the catechizing, with a glance, Regan departed.

"Well, what do you think?" the sheriff asked.

"First," the Ranger replied, "I don't think the fellow was an Arizonan; the rig on his horse is strictly a Texas rig, and even his spurs are not the type usually met with in Arizona and western New Mexico. I'd say he was a Texan."

"And what else?" prompted Serby.

"I think," Slade said slowly, "that it was a case of falling out among thieves. Perhaps he talked too much, or threatened to. Or maybe attempted a little genteel blackmail. Either, or neither, could be the explanation for the shooting. I'd say the gentleman was mixed up with the Starlight Riders and somehow got in bad with the rest of his bunch. So they waited their chances and drygulched him, perhaps because he was pulling out of the section and they figured it was not wise to allow him to run around loose. I sure wish I'd gotten a chance to talk with him before he took the Big Jump. I've a notion I slipped a mite when I didn't try to locate him after the shooting. Although of course he may have died immediately after he rode into the chaparral and fell from his horse."

"Uh-huh, and if you'd gone prowling around in the brush and he was still able to squeeze a trigger, you might have gotten *your* comeuppance. That sort only wounded is dangerous as a broken-back rattler. Suppose he was planted in the Full-House to get the lowdown on things and tip the others off when to act?"

"Possibly." Slade did not commit himself further.

"Well, no matter where he came from, neither Arizona nor Texas lost anything," was the dead man's requiem as voiced by the sheriff.

Serby glanced at the wall clock. "What say we amble back to the office and take a load off our feet for a while?" he suggested. "Soon be time to eat, and I'd sorta like to forget that carcass for a while first. It don't look over nice."

Slade did not differ with him, and they returned to Serby's office. Slade sat down and rolled a cigarette. Serby, as usual, was behind his table-desk. He tugged his mustache, wrinkled his brows. Slade, who read the signs aright, knew that he was turning something over in his mind, and was silent.

Finally the sheriff spoke. "You know," he remarked pensively, "Clay Regan sorta don't look or talk like a jigger who would knuckle under easy to anybody. Seems that jigger we're going to plant was a sorta salty hombre, but it 'pears Regan didn't have any trouble handling him."

Slade remained silent. Serby continued his ruminations.

"Of course," he said, paralleling Slade's tentative reasoning of the night before, "he might have figured it was better business to kick in a mite of blackmail for 'protection' than to buck the bunch."

Slade was noncommittal. "Not beyond the realm of possibility."

Serby shot him a glance. "But you ain't exactly sure that's it, eh?" he said.

Slade spoke slowly. "Regan, undoubtedly being a shrewd businessman, would surely know that their initial demands would be only the beginning. Once they got their claws fixed in him, they would keep on raising the ante until it reached the breaking point, and there would be nothing for him to do but fold up and get out."

"Sounds reasonable," Serby conceded. "Then what's the answer?"

"I don't know, for sure," Slade frankly admitted. "He's a good deal of a puzzler. Of course we could be wrong in our estimate of his shrewdness and saltiness; appearances are sometimes deceptive."

The sheriff jerked his head in the affirmative and continued to tug his mustache. Slade waited expectantly, knowing he had more to say. At length he remarked—

"Maybe he did think of it—that is, if he really knuckled under to them—and has a little scheme of his own for getting out from under. As you said yourself, squash the head of that sort of an outfit and you squash the outfit. Maybe Regan has a notion who the head is and figures to give him his comeuppance."

Slade did not argue. There was a certain logic to the sheriff's reasoning, although it was really more of a theory than reasoning, with no apparent facts upon which to base it. His own vague theory, equally foundationless, he preferred not to discuss at the moment, for it was too much in the nature of a hunch.

But El Halcon had learned from experience not to disregard hunches, so called, which were often a manifestation of sound subconscious marshaling of a series of incidents, each trivial in itself but cumulatively of the greatest importance, requiring only a key happening to resolve them into a readable pattern which would render clear what before had been obscure.

The sheriff shrugged his shoulders, as if dismissing the matter for the time being.

"Let's go eat," he said. Which they proceeded to do. Before they finished, Tomas Cardena joined them.

Sheriff Serby gestured to a chair. "Sorta like our town, eh, Tomas?" he remarked.

"Yes, I do," Cardena replied. "I'm glad of a chance to spend another night here. I have friends with whom I plan to visit. I return to Clint tomorrow, on the noon train."

9

AFTER THE MEAL was finished, Cardena departed to join his *amigos*. The sheriff headed back to his office. Left to his own devices, Slade strolled through the deepening dusk to Pablo Montez' cantina.

Carmen appeared from the back room, where she had been working, in answer to Pablo's call—a shy and blushing Carmen who greeted him with downcast lashes. He crinkled his eyes at her, and the color in her soft cheeks deepened.

"You look wonderful," he complimented her.

She blushed even more rosily, but there was laughter in the big dark eyes when they raised to meet his.

"Well, why shouldn't I?" she replied. "The stars are shining, Uncle Pablo is in a jolly mood, I've finished my book work, and—I won't have to eat my dinner alone. Isn't all that enough to make a girl look satisfied with the immediate present?"

"And the past?"

"Depends on how far back the past goes."

Slade shook his head at the aptness of the retort. She had a quick mind and a delightful sense of humor. He beckoned the waiter who was hovering around, not too close, and ordered in accordance with her suggestions.

"And I'll have coffee with you," he said. "I ate a little while ago."

Carmen shook her head disapprovingly.

"A man of your inches should be hungry all the time," she declared. "Juan," she instructed the waiter, "bring him at least the pie of which Uncle Pablo is so proud. He says that once a man eats his pie he always comes back for more."

The pie was brought, along with the coffee and her dinner. After he had tasted it, Slade was inclined to believe that Pablo might well be right. He made a mental resolve to have another piece later.

Pablo came over to the table, rubbing his hands together complacently.

"Ah," he said. "As it should be. A man has need of his drink, his food and, as you would say, feminine companionship." He chuckled, winked at Slade and sauntered back to the bar.

"The poor dear is so transparent," Carmen observed. "He thinks that with wine, women and song, or what passes for it, he can keep you here and has determined to try."

"Well, he could have a much less laudable ambition. The section grows more and more attractive, day by day and—night by night."

For some reason best known to herself, the apparently inconsequential remark caused Carmen to blush again.

"Song!" she suddenly repeated. "That reminds me. Oh, I've heard about you—'The singingest man in the whole Southwest!' "

She caught the Mexican orchestra leader's eye and beckoned. "Sebastian," she said, "*El Capitan* will sing." She glanced expectantly at Slade.

"Well," he smiled, "I can hardly make a lady a—prevaricator."

Sebastian, with a low bow, led the way to the little raised platform which accommodated the orchestra and handed Slade a guitar. He raised his hand and said simply, "*El Capitan* will sing."

All faces turned toward the platform, and the babble of conversation died to a hum, ceased.

There were quite a number of cowhands present, so Slade first sang a gay old ballad of the rangeland that brought back to his hearers visions of starlit nights, lonely campfires and silences fragrant with the aroma of the prairie grasses.

And as the great metallic baritone-bass pealed through the room, there was a hush that, when the music ended with a crash of chords, was followed by a storm of applause and shouts for another.

In deference to the rivermen who made up a good portion of the crowd, he sang a boating chantey filled with the clash of wave-battling oars, the boom of the sails in an offshore wind and the purling whisper of white water curling under the bow.

Then, with a laughing glance at Carmen, he concluded the performance with a sweet and dreamy love song of Mexico, deftly translated from the Spanish:

> Oh, wings that touch as a fleeting breath!
> Oh, life that births in the arms of death!

Shall souls that walk the starry sky
Pass one another by?
Shall lips meet lips to part?

Out of the night, dream of a dream,
As the silver flight
Of white-winged gulls or the pulsing stream
Of pale moonlight
That bathes the earth in fretted fire,
You came, and the arms of sweet desire
Drew us heart to heart!

There were tears in Carmen's dark eyes when he returned to the table, and she regarded him wistfully.

"I wish it were so," she said.

"Well?"

She shook her head. "Too strong is the call of the open road and the lonely places."

He did not answer.

Quickly, however, her mood changed and laughter replaced tears. She poured him a glass of wine, refilled her own.

"To the present!" she said, and raised her glass.

They drank the toast together, smiling into one another's eyes. Old Pablo beamed.

The cantina was gay and lively with laughter and animated conversations. Admiring glances were cast at the couple at the table, and heads drew together in low-voiced talk.

"They don't come often like that pair," an old waddie declared. "He's one fine-looking man and she's as purty as a spotted dog under a little red wagon. Wonder if they're going to get hitched? They could both do a whole lot worse. I've heard some loco gents say the young feller is an owlhoot. Well, I've a notion we could use a few more owlhoots of that sort hereabouts. Sheriff Serby sure seems to swear by him, and old Trev is hard to fool."

"Right!"

Carmen and Slade had several dances together, during which the other couples edged away to watch their outstanding performance. Both liked to dance, and they could dance. When they returned to their table after the last number, Carmen glanced out the open window.

"It's a beautiful moonlit night," she remarked.

"It is," Slade agreed. "Say! How'd you like to walk across the bridge to Juarez?"

"I'd love it," she answered promptly. "I like Juarez; it is always gay and colorful."

"Let's go," he said.

They waved to Pablo. "We'll be back," Carmen called to him. Pablo waved reply and nodded. As they passed through the swinging doors, he cast a glance at a nearby table.

Slade and Carmen walked slowly, arm in arm. They paused on the crest of the bridge to gaze at the moon-silvered water. The river was a white ribbon of mystery twined in the hair of night. On either side sparkled the lights of Juarez and El Paso. Here on the high bridge they seemed to swing in limitless space between two eternities. Carmen moved closer to him.

"Beautiful!" she murmured. "Oh, time, stand still!"

They continued their slow stroll and soon were on the streets of Juarez. Here life ebbed and flowed at a calmer pace. The air lilted to song and laughter as the simple folk of *Mejico* took their pleasure under the stars. The very buildings spoke of a contentment that hovered close to the earth. Most of the houses were built on the usual Mexican plan, with flat roofs. In poorer homes mud and thatch or reeds did for covering, but there was always room for a garden of gay blossoms and flowering vines.

Juarez' history was as colorful as the town. President Benito Juarez, reformer and national hero, after a desperate but losing battle against thirty thousand French troops of Maximilian, the pretender, was forced to retire to El Paso del Norte, as the town was then called, where he continued to maintain his capital in the face of French invasion. Later the town's name was changed to Juarez in his honor.

Juarez would again know battle and near destruction, but the night Slade and Carmen walked its streets it was a scene of peace. Mexican carftsmen wove rugs and serapes on old-fashioned hand looms. Others displayed hand-tooled leather goods. The markets were vibrant with colors and filled with odors and sounds. Articles ranging from foods to jugs, kettles and mats were to be purchased. There were curio shops, miniature bazaars and numerous cantinas. Also to be had were costly jewelry, rare perfumes, basketware and flowers, and garish souvenirs copied from Aztec art.

There was a subdued strumming of guitars and the songs of wandering troubadours who gathered at street corners, before cafes and in the shadows of the markets to sing the folk songs of old Mexico.

Juarez! Gay, colorful, lethargic, but at times as inflammable as gunpowder!

Slade and Carmen wandered about the streets for quite a while, dropping into several cantinas, in some of which the girl was recognized and greeted.

Finally he said, "Getting late. Guess we'd better amble back across the bridge. You must be tired."

Carmen slanted him a sideways glance, and smiled.

Planking and other building materials were stacked along the bridge rail at intervals.

"Seems they're always making repairs on this darn thing," Slade commented. "It was like this the last time I crossed it."

They were about halfway to the north bank of the river when from not far ahead came a horrible retching scream, followed almost instantly by a sullen splash in the water far below, then another.

Slade halted, shoved Carmen behind him. His hands streaked to his gun butts.

Four forms materialized from the shadows cast by the lumber pile. They paused to glance over the rail, then sauntered forward. Slade watched them, strung for instant action.

"*Amigos, Capitan,*" a voice called.

"That's Gordo Alendes' voice!" Carmen exclaimed thankfully. "He's one of Uncle Pablo's—young men."

Slade relaxed, and they walked on until they met the four.

"What in blazes happened?" the Ranger asked.

Gordo, lean, sinewy, dark-faced, shrugged with Latin eloquence.

"*Loco hombres*—two," he replied. "They go in river. Like to swim by moonlight, *si?*"

Slade drew a deep breath as he noted one of the group was wiping a knife with a handkerchief which he nonchalantly tossed over the rail; Carmen shuddered and snuggled a little closer. Pablo's "young men" were good *amigos,* but they were rather terrible.

"We return," said Gordo and suited the action to the word, he and the others heading toward the north bank at a sprightly pace. Slade and Carmen followed, more slowly.

"What was it, Walt?" the girl asked.

"I think," Slade replied soberly, "that a couple of gents were holed up back of that lumber pile. Gordo and his boys were also holed up nearby, or trailed them."

"They were waiting for you?"

"Possibly," he conceded. "I was thoughtless. I should not have exposed you to danger."

"I don't think there was much danger," she replied calmly. "Am I not with El Halcon, the fearless, the watchful?"

Slade did not believe the drygulchers would have been able to get into action before he spotted them. Just the same he was glad that, thanks to Gordo and his companions, there wasn't a corpse-and-cartridge session; flying lead plays no favorites.

"Feel all right?" he asked his companion.

"Yes, but I think right now I could stand a glass of wine," she replied with a slightly tremulous laugh.

When they reached the cantina, they found that Pablo had reserved their table, on it a fresh bottle of wine. He looked at them as they entered, and shook his head. However, he asked no questions. Doubtless he had already heard the story, for Gordo and the others were seated at another table playing an innocuous game of cards.

Slade filled the glasses from the bottle. Carmen again raised hers.

"Once more, to the present," she said. "At least it is not dull."

"And another to a girl to ride the river with," Slade added. She acknowledged the high compliment with a dazzling smile.

Slade ordered a couple of bottles of wine placed on the table where the card game was in progress, which were received with nods and grins of appreciation.

A little later Pablo smiled, benignly, when they bade him goodnight and left the cantina together.

10

THE FOLLOWING AFTERNOON Slade paid Sheriff Serby a visit and regaled him with an account of the previous night's happenings.

"I think that makes ten, by the latest count," he concluded. "Sort of thinning them out, all right."

"Uh-huh, and we won't be bothered with planting the last two," said Serby. "Pablo's boys are okay.

"But the hellions are still going strong," he added. "A wheat field down the valley a few miles was burned last night."

"The devil you say!" Slade exclaimed.

"Yep, that's right, a sort of new wrinkle. Folks down there have taken to keeping a watch on their buildings and stacks, but I reckon they didn't figure on the fields. Feller who reported it to me said he never saw anything the like. Him and another farmer were keeping an eye on things when all of a sudden the field just seemed to explode with fire. Said it blazed up in every direction and there wasn't a darn thing to do about it. They didn't see anybody, didn't hear anybody, but somebody sure set it."

Slade regarded the sheriff, his eyes thoughtful. "Suppose we take a ride down there and have a look," he suggested

"Not a bad notion," conceded Serby. "Let's go!"

As they rode down the valley, Serby remarked, "They're sure after you hot and heavy."

"Looks sort of that way," Slade agreed cheerfully. "But so far they haven't had anything but bad luck to show for it."

"Here's hoping the luck holds," growled the sheriff. "Seems you can't step out-of-doors without somebody taking a shot at you or something. Sometimes I don't think you've got a nerve in your body. Nothing seems to faze you."

"What's the sense in bothering about what doesn't happen?" Slade pointed out. "If we worry all the time about what might happen, it won't take us long to go loco."

Serby thought that one over and agreed that probably it was so.

They reached the burned field. What had been a fine
stand of wheat was but blackened stubble. A couple of men
who had been watching their approach called a greeting,
came forward to meet them and were introduced to Slade.

"And you say the fire appeared to start in more than one
spot?" the Ranger asked.

"That's right," said one of the farmers. "Seemed to bust
loose everywhere at once. Sort of criss-crossed the field."

"And you neither saw nor heard anybody pass this way on
the trail?"

The farmer shook his head. "The boys have been keeping
watch all along here, up and down," he explained. "They all
said nobody passed this way after dark last night; was
about ten o'clock when the fire started."

Slade nodded and gazed toward the hills beyond the valley,
his eyes thoughtful.

"Suppose we go in and look things over carefully," he
suggested.

"Sartain," said the farmer. He led the way to a gate in
the barbed wire fence and opened it. They passed in and
walked about on the dusty ash.

"Say, what's that over there?" Serby suddenly asked. "Looks
like some sort of burned-up critter."

"Yes," Slade replied quietly, "a coyote."

"Now how the devil did that smart critter get caught in
the fire?" wondered the sheriff.

"I don't think he got *caught* in the fire," Slade replied
dryly. "A coyote is much too smart for that. He would have
hightailed at the first spark, even if he happened to be in the
field, which would be most unusual."

"What the blazes are you getting at?" demanded the
sheriff. "If he didn't get caught by the fire, how did he get
burned up?"

Slade was bending over the crisped body. He pointed to
the animal's tail, of which nothing but bone was left.

"See that length of wire wound around the tail bone?" he
said. "No, the coyote didn't get caught by the fire; he *set*
the fire."

His hearers stared at him as if convinced he had suddenly
gone loco.

"Yes, the coyote set the fire, but not of his own choice,"
Slade repeated. "I encountered something somewhat similar
once before." He straightened up, gazed again toward the
hills and quoted a passage of Scripture—

" 'And Samson went and caught three hundred foxes, and

took firebrands, and turned tail to tail, and put a firebrand in the midst between two tails.

" 'And when he had set the brands on fire, he let them go into the standing corn of the Philistines, and burned up both the shocks, and also the standing corn, with the vineyards and olives.' "

Slade paused, smiling. The old farmer stroked his beard. "Well, I swan!" he exclaimed. "Son, I believe you hit it!"

"Yes, I think I did," Slade said. "It is doubtful if Samson really needed so many foxes. The hellions who burned your field managed to do it with one critter. Trapped a coyote, wired a torch of some kind to his tail, set it alight and tossed the coyote into the wheat field. Of course the poor devil, with his tail afire, tried to run away from the blaze. The fence would balk him, and he'd run in every direction. The wheat, being dry and inflammable, would catch instantly. That's why it seemed to you the fire broke out in every direction at once. A devil's trick for fair, but it worked."

The farmer cut loose with some very creditable profanity, but Sheriff Serby outdid his finest efforts. Slade waited patiently till the outburst had subsided.

"And you are positive nobody passed this way on the trail, after dark?"

"Sure for sartain," the farmer insisted. Slade nodded and turned to once more gaze at the hills.

The farmers gazed at *him*. "Son, you're smart, plumb smart," said the elder of the pair, a taciturn individual who had not spoken a word since the initial greeting. "Yep, plumb smart. And you're after those skuts, too?"

"Well, they've tried to kill me a few times," Slade replied.

The old farmer nodded. "Don't make you over fond of 'em, I guess. One of your deputies, Sheriff?"

"Well, he has been," Serby replied, with truth.

"Good!" said the farmer, who evidently took the sheriff's evasive reply for an affirmative. "Good! He'll get 'em."

Slade smiled. "I hope your confidence isn't misplaced," he said.

"It ain't," declared the farmer. "Son, I callate to know hogs and cows, and men. You'll get 'em."

"Thank you," Slade said. "Well, Trevis, I guess we might as well head back to town. Nothing more to do down here, at the moment."

"Reckon so," the sheriff agreed. "Be seeing you, boys, and hope to have good news for you 'fore long."

As they rode for El Paso, Serby remarked, "Those old fellers are okay. Smart, too."

"Down East stock, endowed with native New England shrewdness," Slade replied. Serby shot him a curious glance. "How you figure they're Down East?" he asked.

"Very seldom do you hear such expressions as 'I swan' and 'callate' anywhere outside of New England," Slade explained. Serby shook his head. "Ever miss anything?"

"I came close to doing just that last night," Slade answered. "I was careless, and had it not been for Gordo and his bunch I might well have run into trouble."

"A purty gal alongside a young feller is liable to make him forget everything else," the sheriff commented wisely.

"You may have something there," Slade admitted with a smile. "I've a notion, though, that she would have spotted those two devils before I did; she seemed to see everything."

"It's the woman who spots trouble first," nodded Serby. "She figures the interpolper 'fore the man realizes he's being tangled up. She's always on the lookout to protect her man."

Slade nodded sober agreement; there was truth in the old peace officer's reasoning.

During the ride back to town, Serby chattered garrulously, but Slade was mostly silent, his replies distrait, for he was thinking deeply.

That night he translated his thoughts into action. In the dead dark hours just before the dawn, he rode west on the Valley Trail. After he was beyond the last straggle of the town, after a long pause to study the back track and make sure he was not being followed, he turned north by east, skirting Comanche Peak and traversing the rough and broken ground that edged the valley. Full daylight found him in the beginning of the hills.

On an elevation he drew rein, rolled a cigarette and sat gazing at the green and gold beauty of the valley basking in the morning sunlight.

"Horse," he said, "those farmers were positive that nobody rode the trail night before last when the field was burned. So it's logical to believe the devils slid down from the hills by a way where there were no watchman stationed, to fire the wheat. And I think it's also logical to believe that they have a hangout somewhere in the hills from which they can conduct operations without attracting attention. Outlaw procedure usually follows a fairly uniform pattern. Anyhow, for a while we're going to work in accordance with that presumption. If we can locate their hangout, assuming that they really have one somewhere in the foothills, we'll be a long ways toward smashing the outfit. I've a sort of notion, although it could be way off, as to just who is the big he-wolf of the pack. Our chore is to get the lowdown on him, which isn't likely to be easy; I figure him to be a shrewd article. Well, we'll see."

He pinched out his cigarette and rode on into the hills.

11

SLADE WAS NOT riding aimlessly. The hills were steep, rugged and heavily brush grown, but he felt confident that somewhere was an easy route by which they could be penetrated. He quartered the ground back and forth, estimating the distance from El Paso and the valley, the approachableness of the terrain. The Starlight Riders were aptly named, for they undoubtedly did most of their raiding under the cover of darkness. Which meant that there *must* be a fairly easy route. Horsemen could not, with any degree of success, negotiate the thorny and rocky slopes in the gloom of night.

It took him a long time—the sun was well up the slant of the eastern sky, but finally he found it, a faint and, to an extent, overgrown track winding upward. Doubtless it had originally been an old Indian trail followed by raiding parties of Apaches or Comanches. Used later perhaps by hunters and prospectors. For the hills of Texas and New Mexico knew many ancient, now deserted, cabins and shacks once occupied by those wanderers. One of which very likely had been commandeered by the outlaws, probably no distance from the old trail. He followed its windings into the heart of the hills.

He grew exultant as a close examination of occasional soft spots in the surface of the trail revealed that indubitably horses had passed that way, going and coming. It was possible, of course, that cowhands from the northern ranches used the old track as a short cut, but that he thought unlikely, the hoof prints not being abundant enough to indicate steady traffic by large numbers of horses over an extended period. More and more he leaned to the belief that his hunch was a straight one and that he was actually on the track of the outlaw band.

Now, he rode warily, paying particular attention to the actions of his feathered friends, the birds, for there was no telling what he might encounter in these gloomy fastnesses. Also, the cabin or shack, were there really one, might be well hidden in the dense growth. He could easily pass it by were he not watchful. Mostly the surface of the trail was hard and stony and did not retain the impress of horses' irons—there were long stretches where none were visible, in the course of which he scanned the brush on either side with the greatest care, searching for telltale broken twigs or branches stripped of leaves, which would be evidence of horsemen pushing their way through the growth.

And he constantly scanned the sky for that indubitable indication of human occupancy—smoke.

But the heavens remained stainless blue, with only the chirping of birds in the thickets and the sounding of a gentle breeze through the branches to break the peaceful hush of the wastelands. He was now well into the hills and was beginning to wonder if his hunch really *was* a straight one, for he felt that the hangout, if there was one, would not be too far from the valley.

However, all things come to him who waits, and sometimes to him who doesn't. Suddenly El Halcon's acute hearing was conscious of a sound, faint but persistent, and steadily loudening. The beat of hoofs drumming the hard surface of the trail. Coming not from in front but from behind, in the direction of the sharp bend he had just rounded.

Fortunately, at this point the growth was thinner than average and he was able to force Shadow into the thorny tangle far enough for both horse and rider to be concealed. Tense and expectant, he peered through a slight rift in the screen of leafy branches.

Around the bend bulged three horsemen, riding at a fast clip. Slade caught a glimpse of hard-lined faces and eyes glinting in the shadow of low-drawn hat brims as they whisked past and continued out of sight on the curving trail. All three were big, bulky men, well mounted. Because of the obscuring leaves, fluttering in the breeze, he was unable to get more than a blurred distortion of their features, but it seemed to him that one, riding slightly in front, looked familiar, although it was possibly just a trick of his imagination.

He waited a few moments, then eased Shadow out of the growth. For several minutes more he sat listening and watching the bend in the trail. Then he gathered up the reins.

"We'll just amble along and see if we can find out who those gents are and where they're headed for," he told the horse. "They could be just some harmless cowhands, but I've a feeling they're not. And I also can't help but feel that somewhere, sometime, I saw the one before. Sort of struck me that I should remember him, that I'd seen him recently, though where or under what circumstances I haven't the slightest notion. Well, let's go, and maybe we will learn something."

He sent Shadow drifting along at a fair pace, now and then reining in to listen. But no untoward sound broke the silence. The trail wound on in the blaze of the noonday sun, and he saw nothing.

Constantly he scanned the growth on either side for signs of passage through it and discovered none. Nowhere was an indication of horses forcing their way into the tangle. He had covered the better part of a mile when he came to a short stretch of soft trail. He dismounted and examined the ground, then quickly remounted. Yes, the three riders were still ahead. With almost another mile of slow going he began to wonder if the horsemen were not really just chance travelers heading for some distant point. Began to look that way.

"But, blast it! I still don't think so," he told Shadow, who blew softly through his nose as if in agreement.

Another quarter of a mile, with the sun slanting westward and the branches casting traceries of dusty gold on the shadowy surface of the trail, and abruptly their continued faith was justified, the hunch proved to be a straight one.

Smoke! Slade didn't see it, but he smelled it—the fragrant whiff of wood smoke borne on the fluttery wings of the wind. And from no great distance ahead. Somebody had kindled a fire of dry wood.

Instantly Slade reined in and sat peering and listening. He could hear no sound, could see no signs of movement in the brush, but the woody tang grew stronger. After another moment of hesitation, he sent Shadow ahead again, at a slow walk.

"We're getting close," he muttered, "darn close." He began scanning the growth on the right side of the trail, from whence the smell came. A few more yards and the brush thinned a little.

"This should do, feller," he whispered. "We'll ease in there and I'll leave you for a while. And for Pete's sake, be quiet!"

Without argument, Shadow sidled into the chaparral. Only a short distance from the trail was a little open patch where there was a scanty growth of grass that the big black evidently thought inviting, for as soon as Slade flipped the bit from his mouth he began to graze.

Easy in his mind, because Shadow was usually a very quiet horse, Slade glided through the growth toward the source of the smoke, the smell of which grew stronger as he advanced, now mingled with the enticing aroma of frying meat and boiling coffee. He was not at all surprised when the growth thinned and, peering through a final leafy screen, he saw a weatherbeaten but stanch-appearing cabin set in a little clearing. Around the clearing were scattered the desiccating skeletons of animals. Evidently the place had been the home of a trapper and hunter in the days when the hills teemed with game.

There was nobody in sight, but under a ramshackle lean-to stood three horses, their rigs removed, munching oats from feed boxes. Apparently their owners were in the cabin preparing a meal.

Relaxing comfortably, Slade pondered the situation. The three riders, he reasoned, had, like himself, left El Paso before daybreak. Why were they here? A rendezvous with other members of the bunch? Or was the cabin the base from which to start some marauding expedition, doubtless directed at the inhabitants of the valley? He earnestly wished he could get a look into the cabin, but present circumstances made such an attempt highly inadvisable. He'd just have to take it easy and await developments.

They were slow in coming. Listening intently, he could hear sounds from inside the cabin. A mutter of voices, the scrape of a pushed-back chair, a tinny rattle that was probably somebody setting a table. Smoke curled slowly from the stick-and-mud chimney. Now and then a shadow would pass one of the dusty windows, the panes of which were still intact.

The cabin gave the impression of having frequently known recent occupancy. Slade was pretty well convinced that he had discovered the hidden hangout of the Starlight Riders. But what to do with it now that he had found it, he was hanged if he knew. Yes, nothing to do at the moment but wait and see which way the cat jumped. Having had considerable experience with that mythical feline, he knew it to be most unpredictable.

A tedious hour passed, another, and a good part of a third, and Slade grew heartily sick of the continued inactivity. But there wasn't a darned thing he could do about that, either. To attempt to get the drop on the three occupants of the cabin would be the act of a stark, staring lunatic, to put it mildly. Besides, there was the chance that he would be making a ludicrous blunder. No law that he ever heard of against folks occupying a deserted cabin, possibly with a perfectly legitimate reason for doing so. In his mind he was convinced that the trio were members of the Starlight Riders, but being convinced in his mind and being sure were totally different matters. He'd just have to wait. If three men planned to spend the night in the cabin, under cover of darkness he might be able to learn something definite. If they were just waiting for darkness to start out on some venture, he'd try to learn what that venture was and, if it seemed advisable, endeavor to thwart it. Nothing to do but wait.

12

Now the sun was slanting down the western sky, and twilight was not so far off. Slade shifted from one uncomfortable position to another—all positions had become uncomfortable—and swore wearily, under his breath.

And then, abruptly, business picked up. From the growth beyond the cabin, which flanked the trail, rode two men. One raised his voice in a shout that was answered by a call within the cabin. They proceeded to the lean-to, dismounted, flipped out their mounts' bits and poured oats into feed boxes. They did not remove the rigs. Those matters attended to, they repaired to the cabin. Slade could not get a very good look at their faces, but neither appeared familiar. One man was lean and lanky, the other not so tall but broader. They vanished from his sight and had evidently entered the cabin.

The muttering rumble of voices loudened. Again there was a rattling, as of tin plates and cups. Smoke rose from the chimney. Apparently a meal was being prepared for the newcomers. Slade schooled himself to patience and further waiting. Now the sun had set, and the clearing was growing shadowy.

A light flared in the cabin, and he wondered gloomily if he was doomed to an all-night vigil. However, he deemed this unlikely, due to the fact that the new arrivals had not divested their horses of saddle and bridle. Looked like they expected to shortly be on the move. Slade devoutly hoped his reasoning was sound.

It was. The clearing was gloomy with the dusk when, after considerable sounds of activity, the light in the cabin was extinguished. Another moment and the five men filed out and headed for the lean-to. To Slade's disgust it was already too dark to make anything of their features. A few more minutes and they rode across the clearing toward the brush which flanked the trail. Slade glided noiselessly to where Shadow awaited him.

He heard the bunch ride past his hiding place, in the di-

rection of the valley. After a short period of waiting he led
Shadow to the trail and mounted.

Now El Halcon found himself in a quandary. If he got too
close to the dubious quintet and they heard him coming, he
might well be blown from under his hat. And if he let them
get too far ahead, he might lose them.

Such was the horned dilemma upon one point or other of
which he ran the risk of being impaled. He considered the
matter with an earnestness that almost amounted to mental
agony. Once the quarry reached the open ground at the end
of the old trail, he would have no difficulty keeping them in
sight. That is, if he didn't let them get too far ahead.

"Well, horse, we'll just have to take a chance," he said.
Estimating the speed at which the five were traveling and
hoping he was making no mistake, he sent Shadow easing
down the trail in their wake.

It was a nerve-straining business, riding the winding
trail through the black dark. The moon had not yet risen,
and only the faintest glimmer of starlight seeped through the
overhanging growth. Slade strained his ears to catch any sound
from in front. He was fairly confident that he would hear
the beat of hoofs ahead before Shadow's soft tread would be
caught by listening ears. But if the bunch halted for some reason or other—well, the less he considered that possibility, the
better. A hand close to a gun butt, he held to a steady pace.

The miles flowed back. The silver edge of the moon had
appeared in the east, he knew by the brightening of the sky.
Shouldn't be quite so dark after a bit.

The miles and the hours passed; it was not so very far
from midnight, and the valley should now be fairly close.
Twice Slade was sure he heard a faint clicking of hoofs ahead.
Each time he paused to listen, then rode on, reassured that
the quarry was still but a reasonable distance ahead.

Finally he reached the point where the old trail merged
with the open but unproductive land which edged the
valley. Keeping back in the shadow, he swept the terrain
with his eyes and spotted the quarry, little more than three
hundred yards ahead, riding south by east.

Slade relaxed comfortably. Now he was freed of personal
danger, the advantage was his. His long-range Winchester
plus Shadow's great speed and endurance rendered him safe
from the threat of the lopsided odds. All he had to do now
was keep the quintet in sight without being spotted himself. And with his own extraordinary keen vision, he was
confident he could do just that. Lounging in the saddle,

he waited until they were but moving blobs in the watery moonlight that seeped through the thin clouds of a slightly overcast sky. Then he sent Shadow drifting along in their wake.

Where the devil were they headed for and what were they up to, he wondered. They were steadily edging toward the houses and cultivated fields of the farmlands. Figured to set another field afire? Best as he recalled, the one that was burned was the only wheat field in the immediate section. Alfalfa, potatoes, onions and grapes were not good fodder for the arsonist.

Abruptly the riders turned almost due south, toward a narrow but long belt of thicket. In the distance, beyond the thicket, Slade could make out the dark bulk of a big farmhouse. A little later he recognized it as the one belonging to the two old farmers who had defied the Starlight Riders and whose field was burned. Well, the two old gents, in a thoroughly bad temper, would be keeping a close watch over their property, and if the hellions intended to make a try for the house, they'd quite likely meet with a reception they wouldn't enjoy. Slade increased Shadow's speed. He wanted to be in on the shindig when it started. Abruptly he straightened in the saddle and stared.

The group had split up. Two were riding at a swift pace parallel to the belt of thicket. The other three, more slowly, still continued straight toward the growth. Shortly they vanished into it. The other two were now shadowy in the distance. They, too, vanished from his sight.

Several minutes passed, with the somewhat bewildered Ranger approaching the thicket. What in the devil were the hellions up to, anyhow?

Then suddenly from the point where the speeding pair had disappeared from sight came a crackle of shots and a wild yelling. Again and again the unseen guns boomed. And abruptly Slade understood. The pair were creating a diversion. Every farmer around would race toward where it appeared a blazing gunfight was under way between their neighbors and the outlaws. The big farmhouse would be left unguarded, for the two old farmers lived alone, with the other devils free to work their will on it. By the time the farmers realized what was happening, the building would be on fire and doomed.

Slade's voice rang out—"Trail, Shadow, trail!"

Instantly the great black extended himself, racing toward the belt of thicket at top speed. Slade knew he was taking a chance, but he counted on the three's attention being directed in the other direction. If it wasn't . . .

He didn't hesitate. Bending low in the saddle, he sent Shadow surging on. With a breath of relief, he reached the growth, crashed through it to the other side and spotted the three outlaws, on foot and running toward the farmhouse; they were less than two hundred yards distant.

They heard and saw him coming, as he knew they would, and whirled about. Slade whipped the Winchester from the saddle boot as guns flashed and bullets stormed past, uncomfortably close. His voice rang out again—

"Easy, Shadow!"

The black leveled off to a smooth running-walk. Slade's eyes glanced along the sights. The rifle bucked against his shoulder as fire streamed from its muzzle.

One of the outlaws threw up his hands and pitched headlong. Answering bullets ripped the sleeve of Slade's shirt, drilled the crown of his hat.

Again the gray eyes glancing along the sights. Again the gush of orange flame. A second arsonist reeled and fell. The one remaining raced forward, shooting as he came. Slade swayed far sideways and fired under Shadow's neck, Comanche fashion. Again and again he pulled trigger, the ejecting lever a flashing blur.

The outlaw halted as if struck by a mighty fist. For an instant he stood erect, then slowly toppled to the ground. Slade halted his mount and glanced at the three motionless forms. He raised his eyes and spotted the other two, far in the distance, racing their horses toward the hills. No sense in trying to run them down; they'd be in the clear long before he could hope to overtake them, even were it advisable to try and do so. Once in the growth of the slopes, the advantage would be all theirs.

Men were running toward him, volleying questions. Slade waved his hand and stayed right where he was, hoping that some trigger-nervous farmer wouldn't figure that tonight any head that showed should be whacked.

First to reach him were the two old farmers who owned the building. They gave whoops of recognition.

"So it's you, son!" bawled the elder, his taciturnity all of a sudden gone. "Might have knowed it! Might have knowed it! Didn't I say you'd get 'em? Didn't I say you'd get 'em? How come you happened along at just the right time?"

"I saw them come out of the hills," Slade replied briefly. "It was a smart try and almost worked."

"Not smart enough, though," chortled the oldster. "Not with you on the job. Son, put 'er there! We're mighty obliged to you."

Smiling, Slade "put 'er there." Others crowded around to shake his hand and shower him with congratulations.

Lanterns were brought, the bodies examined. "Ornery-look ing scuts," growled the old farmer.

Slade was disappointed that none of the three was the big man who had looked familiar.

"Let's see what they have on them," he suggested, mindful of the slip of paper taken from the pocket of one of the train wreckers.

However, nothing of significance was revealed other than a sizeable sum of money.

"Guess that should be your bounty on the pelts, son," chuckled the old farmer.

Slade smilingly shook his head and handed him the dinero. "Will pay, partly at least, for your wheat field," he said. The old fellow started to protest, but a glance at Slade's face changed his mind. With a grin, he pocketed the bills and coin.

"And now come on in for a drink and something to eat," he invited.

"Thanks very much, but I'm heading for town," Slade replied. "Folks there who'll be worried about me, and I want to notify the sheriff of what happened, so he can come down and collect the bodies. By the way, you should find three saddled and bridled horses somewhere in the brush over there. Tie onto them, too, they're good cayuses. Be seeing you."

13

WHEN HE ARRIVED at El Paso, Slade made sure his horse was properly cared for and then repaired to the sheriff's office where, as he expected, although it was well past midnight, he found Serby waiting for him.

"Figured you'd turn up sooner or later," the sheriff said. He glanced at Slade's ripped shirtsleeve and the bullet-punctured crown of his hat.

"Been at it again, eh? What happened this time?"

Slade told him, briefly, for he was getting a bit tired. Serby let go a few pungent remarks.

"I'll ride down there with a wagon in the morning," he said. "Now what?"

"Now I'm going down to Pablo's cantina for something to eat," Slade replied. "Guess I'd better wash up first, though."

"Wash up after you get there," the sheriff advised. "I think the little gal down there is developing a bad case of jitters. Two of Pablo's boys were here a little while ago, asking for you. I told them I figured you'd show up here, sooner or later, and I expect they're hanging around outside somewhere, to make sure you get to Pablo's place okay. I figure she sent 'em."

"Wouldn't be surprised," Slade admitted. "By the way, keep that cabin and the old trail under your hat. I merely told the farmers that I saw the devils come out of the hills, which was true. They were too excited to ask for details. I don't think the pair that escaped knew I tailed them through the hills. Doubtless they figured I was holed up in the thicket. Knowledge of the cabin might prove of value sometime. I think it serves as a base of operations, from which they start their marauding expeditions, at least part of the time."

"You figure we might catch 'em in the cabin?"

"Have to do better than that," Slade answered. "Just the fact that they'd be holed up in the cabin wouldn't be enough; we still wouldn't have anything on them. But if we managed to trail them from one of their depredations it would be a different matter. There's an old saying, 'knowledge learned is power earned.' Might apply in this instance."

"Figure you're right there," agreed the sheriff. "Well, see you tomorrow—today, rather, it's way past midnight."

Slade chuckled to himself as he walked to Pablo's cantina, for he had at once spotted the two "young men" Carmen sent to look for him. They were capable trackers and good at keeping out of sight, but they lacked El Halcon's eyes, his meticulous noting of all details and his ability to divine men's intentions from their movements. The *muchachos* strolled casually, a bit too casually. Not with the stealthy, purposeful tread of men with a definite objective in view.

Nevertheless, Slade knew, they would instantly spot anybody trying to close in on him and swing into grim action. So he continued on his way with a carefree mind.

Carmen had the jitters, all right. "I was becoming utterly frantic when you didn't show up for dinner and then didn't show up at all. You told me you didn't expect to be gone so very long."

"I didn't expect to, but I sort of got delayed," he replied.

"Tell me about it," she urged. "What happened?"

"Okay," he answered, "on the condition that what the ear hears, the heart shall keep to itself alone."

"Don't worry," she replied. "I won't talk."

He told her, in detail. She shuddered at his description of the battle by the farmhouse.

"What a life you lead!" she sighed. "Always you are in danger."

"Aren't we all, and all the time?" he countered. "Nobody knows what the next minute has in store."

"Yes, I guess that is so," she conceded. Her bright smile flashed out, and she raised her glass.

"As before," she said, "to the present! It's all we have, and we'll make the most of it. Here come Gordo and Manuel. I told them not to come back without you. And now I'm having an extra-special dinner prepared for you. I'm going to the kitchen to make sure everything is as it should be."

"I'll wash up and then do full justice to it," he promised. Which he did.

Pablo came over and chatted with them a few minutes, but asked no questions. Gordo and Manuel replied to Slade's smile and nod with their usual grins and turned their attention back to their eternal card game.

After Slade had finished his coffee and after-dinner ciga-

rette, Carmen said, "It's very late. You have things to do
tomorrow. Shall we go? You must be very tired."

It was Slade's turn to smile.

There was more than a little excitement in El Paso the
following afternoon when the sheriff arrived with the bodies.
A number of the farmers accompanied him, and the story
of what had happened quickly spread all over town. The
coroner's office was soon jammed with the curious.

This time several bartenders and a couple of shopkeepers
recalled seeing the three men but vouchsafed no knowledge
of them or their activities.

"I think those fellers are telling the truth," Serby said to
Slade. "You've broken the hellions' grip on the section, and
people ain't afraid to talk anymore. About time for somebody to really tell us something."

"I hope so," Slade replied, "for the chore is still a long
ways from being completed."

"Anyhow, you're sure thinning them out," said Serby.
"About a dozen so far, best as I figure. Can't be many left."

"Not so sure about that," Slade differed. "Hard to tell
how big an organization like this can be. Over in Arizona,
Brocius could get together a hundred men if he happened to
want them, or so it was said. The same applied to Kingfisher
and others here in Texas. However, I don't think this outfit is anything like that large, although there may be still
quite a few of them left, including the head or heads of the
organization."

"And they," the sheriff observed, "must be getting just a
mite jittery; things haven't been going so good for them since
you coiled your twine in the section."

"I've been getting some very efficient assistance," Slade
replied, with a smile. "You and Carmen and Pablo and his
bunch have been nicely lending a hand. And the farmers
are cooperating well. All you need to do is get folks properly
riled, and right prevails."

"Uh-huh, if somebody happens along with the nerve and
the personality to get 'em riled," grunted Serby.

"I sure wish I'd gotten a better look at the one who appeared familiar," Slade remarked thoughtfully. "Somehow I
have a feeling that he's the big he-wolf of the pack."

"Didn't notice anything peculiar about him that might give
you a clue?"

"Only the way he sat his horse," Slade replied. "Rigid,
upright, shoulders squared. His seat more that of a cavalryman

than a range rider. I sort of subconsciously noticed that. Really didn't think of it until later. In fact, I think it impressed on me when they rode away from the clearing in the dusk. I didn't get a glimpse of his face, but I did have a good view of his back."

"Might mean something," observed Serby.

"Yes, it might," Slade agreed. "A small detail, but small details are sometimes significant."

"You've sure proved that often enough," said the sheriff. "Here's hoping you get a good look at that gent riding down Texas Street. Now what?"

"Darned if I know," Slade replied cheerfully. "Think I'll go out and wander around a bit; it's a nice evening. Maybe I'll get an inspiration."

"If you don't stop wandering around that blasted riverfront at night, you're liable to get something that won't be inspiring," growled the sheriff.

"Breaks the monotony," Slade said as he headed for the door.

"I could stand a mite of peaceful monotony for a change," grunted Serby. "Oh, why did I ever stop following a cow's tail!"

Slade laughed and departed.

Although it was not yet dark, Slade did finally wander to the waterfront, toward that tract known as the Chamizal Zone which embraced a part of South El Paso.

The Rio Grande, the accepted-by-treaty dividing line between the United States and Mexico, was to a rather large extent responsible for the international tone of El Paso because of its tendency to change its course at will. It fostered the mixing of nationalities by cutting off large slices from Mexico and putting them in Texas in return for Texas lands transferred to Mexico.

A prime example was the Chamizal Zone, a tract of some six hundred acres extending eastward to Cordova Island. An international dispute over the section was based on controversy regarding the cause of the river's changed course. The row appeared to be endless.

As he neared the section, which showed many vacant stretches, Slade noted activity on one of the open spaces. A surveyor with a transit was taking sights on a surveyor's rod with its graduated numbers, which was held by an assistant. Nearby, apparently directing operations, was a big, well-dressed man with an impassive face and keen dark eyes whom Slade at once recognized as Bruce Parker, the promoter and real estate man.

Parker noted his approach and waved his hand. "Laying out the site of one of the hotels I propose to erect," he said as Slade drew near.

"Yes?" Slade replied.

"Yes. An ideal site with a splendid view and near the river. I am dickering for the land, which I can get almost for nothing. Couldn't be better."

Slade nodded, but did not otherwise comment. It was none of his business; Parker had a right to build wherever it pleased him to do so.

But on this disputed tract claimed by two countries, the argument over which might be settled either way, might be ended tomorrow or might go on for years—which it did!—it was impossible for Parker to know just where he stood. No telling where he might find his hotel by the time it was completed. Well, it was his business.

Parker had turned his attention back to the surveyor, who had just repeated a measurement called by his assistant with the rod.

"Just a minute," Parker said. "Let me take that sight over. Didn't sound just right to me."

He expertly adjusted the transit, moving one leg of the tripod a little and slightly changing the alignment of the telescope, and took a sight. He called the number as intercepted between the two horizontal spider lines on the reticle. The rodman called the repeat.

Parker stepped away from the instrument. "That's better," he said to the surveyor. "Evidently you didn't quite hear what the rodman said; you differed with him. Okay, go ahead. You're all set now.

"Have to keep an eye on those fellows," he added in low tones to Slade. "They get careless and may end up in a property-line dispute."

"I see," Slade replied vaguely, as if he did not "see" at all but was willing to take Parker's word for it. He chatted for a few minutes, the promoter pointing out salient features of the site and their advantages. Then he left and retraced his steps back toward the main town, the concentration furrow deep between his black brows, a sure sign El Halcon was doing some hard thinking.

Once he turned to gaze back at Parker's stalwart, soldierly-erect figure. Abruptly he changed direction and headed for the International Bridge. He mounted to its crest and leaned against the rail, gazing absently at the tawny flood of the Rio Grande.

" 'There's a divinity that shapes our ends, Rough-hew them how we will,' " he quoted to the hurrying water. "Strange the part chance plays! Or is it chance? Rather, the inscrutable workings of a Law that says, 'Hitherto shalt thou come, but no further!' "

He turned from the river and walked slowly back to town.

14

LATER, SLADE REMARKED to Sheriff Serby, "Understand Bruce Parker plans to build a hotel down in the Chamizal Zone."

"That's right," said Serby, "He's been sounding off about it. Gather quite a few folks are puzzled over his choice of a site, but I reckon he knows what he's doing."

"Yes, I think he does precisely," Slade replied.

The sheriff looked slightly puzzled, but the Ranger did not elaborate on his remark.

The coroner had been busy all afternoon, and it was nearly dark when the inquest was held on the bodies of the slain outlaws.

It was brief. Slade was commended on doing a good chore; regret was expressed that two of the sidewinders had managed to get away. The sheriff was advised to run them down as quickly as possible. After which everybody repaired to the place on Texas Street for a snort and something to eat.

After finishing his meal, Slade strolled to the stable to make sure Shadow was okay.

"Well, horse," he said, "beginning to look like things are tieing up. Not that the knot—and I'm *not* trying to make a pun—is anything like tight yet. Seven turns to a hangman's knot, they say. I figure we've got maybe two turns, so far. Five turns to go.

"But," he added, "chances are that before the chore is finished, the old saying, 'Judge Colt holds court on the Rio Grande,' is more likely to come true. Well, we'll see.

"Not a great deal to go on so far, horse. Just a phony fight in a saloon, a few lines drawn on a slip of paper, a pair of overalls and a shirt stuffed with straw, the way a man sits his horse, and a couple of chance meetings. No, not much, but something, and we've made out with less.

"And not to be discarded, a chuck-line-riding cowhand who took to a crooked trail, lost his nerve, and eventually his life. *He* might well be the master thread that will unravel the whole web. For it was him gave me my first real notion."

Leaving the stable, he wandered around town a bit. He could always think best in the open air, and he figured he had plenty to think about. Somehow he must try to anticipate the next move the bunch would make and, if possible, forestall it. He was inclined to agree with Sheriff Serby that those remaining were getting a mite jittery. If so, it was not unlikely that they would grow a bit too reckless and pull something that would tip their hand.

That, however, was too problematical to be relied upon. And, if possible, he preferred to take the initiative. He reasoned it was logical to believe another attempt would be made to get rid of him. And the "hired hands" having signally failed, the head of the outfit might decide to take over the chore. Which would probably mean something subtle and original.

For as a rule, owlhoot outfits quickly realized that trying to drygulch El Halcon in any of the accepted manners was a senseless and frequently fatal waste of time.

Well, if something was tried, it might provide the opportunity he needed. He strolled on with a carefree mind.

Abruptly he arrived at a decision. Take the initiative? Okay, he'd take it. He turned his steps toward the riverfront, walking the dark streets warily, shooting glances in every direction, his eyes missing nothing. Finally he turned a corner, passed the dark alley and reached Stanton Street. Without hesitating, he entered the Full-House, strolled to the bar and ordered a drink.

The bartender smiled and nodded. Slade watched closely as he poured the drink and saw nothing out of the ordinary. Raising the full glass to his lips he sniffed sharply. If the liquor was drugged, he'd know it at once.

It wasn't; it was darn good whiskey. He sipped it, his gaze roving over the fairly well-crowded room. Nobody paid him the slightest attention.

Clay Regan sauntered up to the bar. "How are you, Mr. Slade?" he greeted. "Understand you did another good chore last night. Keep up the good work." He motioned to the bartender.

"Have one on the house," he invited.

Again Slade watched the drink poured. It came from the same bottle as the first one. The glass the bartender rinsed, turning it upside down before filling it.

"Thank you, Mr. Regan," Slade said. "If you don't mind,

I'll take this one over to that vacant table by the dance floor. Feeling a mite tired."

"Certainly, certainly," Regan replied. "Make yourself comfortable." With a nod he strolled back to the far end of the bar. Slade sat down at the table, the filled glass before him. He had an excellent view of the swinging doors, and of the room reflected in the backbar mirror. He sipped his drink. Still nobody paid him any mind; nothing happened.

The waiter who had served him during his previous visit approached. Slade ordered coffee and a piece of pie.

"Remember that fellow we were talking about the other night, the one who quit?" the waiter asked. "Heard he was picked up dead in the brush down to the south. Guess he got his bristles up with the wrong party."

"Looks sort of that way," Slade conceded.

The coffee and the pie were brought. He sampled both and found nothing to complain of. The recklessness of his mood was increasing. Resolved to go all out, he had a couple of dances with a dance floor girl who really wasn't bad. If anything was contemplated, now was the time for it. A man with his arms full of woman is at a disadvantage. Nothing happened. He began experiencing a feeling of frustration. After buying the girl a couple of drinks at the table and slipping her a bill, he ordered another cup of coffee, which he drank slowly. After which he gave up, so far as the Full-House was concerned.

Waving goodnight to Regan, he left the place, sweeping the street with an all-embracing glance as he stepped out the door. Nobody in sight. He turned the corner and approached the dark alley mouth, probing its gloom with his eyes. It was silent and empty. He shrugged and walked on, slowly, along the deserted street. If anybody had notions, now was the opportunity to put them into effect.

Apparently nobody had notions; nothing happened. The sense of frustration was growing. He walked on. Everything remained peaceful. He reached a better lighted street, turned a corner. Here quite a few people were going about their business, paying him no mind. Thoroughly disgusted with the whole episode, he headed for Pablo's cantina in a decidedly disgruntled mood. Undoubtedly he had been neatly outsmarted. The hellions had not come to the lure. Evidently they were shrewder than he had given them credit for being. He glowered at the lights, which had not offended in any way.

Then his sense of humor came to the rescue and he chuckled.

He felt like a little boy caught slipping a frog into the teacher's desk drawer. Oh, well, maybe the "frog" wouldn't get away next time.

Abruptly, for no good reason so far as he could see, a feeling of uneasiness swept over him, and instantly he was very much on the alert.

In men who ride much alone with danger as a constant stirrup companion, there births a subtle sixth sense that warns of peril when none, apparently, is near. In El Halcon that sense was strongly developed. He saw nothing, heard nothing that could be classed as inimical, but the voiceless monitor in his brain was setting up a clamor. And he had learned not to disregard that imperative warning. He slowed his pace as he turned a corner. Looked like his invisible guardian had for once made a mistake. Pablo's cantina was now less than a block away.

As he drew near the cantina, he noted two men across the street, almost opposite the cantina door, who appeared to be having a violent argument, for they waved their hands threateningly and fumbled at each other.

Lining the street, set at strategic points, were big whiskey barrels filled with water, a safeguard against fire, which was a prevalent threat in this neighborhood of ramshackle buildings. Slade always eyed those barrels closely when approaching them, for their bulk would provide concealment for a man lurking behind one. There was one only a couple of yards distant as he neared the door. He spared it a swift glance, returned his gaze to the two disputants across the street, who apparently were absorbed in their own discussion.

He saw the pair whirl toward him, caught a gleam of shifted metal and dived headlong for the shelter of the barrel as the guns blazed.

A slug yelled past. Another chunked solidly into the barrel, and still another. He thrust a Colt around the bulge of the barrel and sprayed the opposite side of the street with bullets.

A yelp of pain echoed the reports, then a thud of running feet. He tensed to meet the attack, then realized that the sound was fading away from him. Peering cautiously around the barrel, he saw that the drygulchers—one lagging behind, his right arm flopping grotesquely by his side—were almost to the far corner. He sent two slugs whining after them, but the range was great for a sixgun, and the next instant they whisked around the corner and out of sight. He holstered his Colt and straightened up.

Yes, he had been outsmarted, all right. The pair, with

consummate daring, had chosen the very spot where he was most likely to be careless. Only that uncanny sense that warned of impending danger, plus the convenient water barrel and his perfect coordination of brain and muscle, had saved him.

Heads were poking cautiously out the door, calling questions.

"Two jiggers went around the corner over there, one in front of the other," Slade replied evasively, leaving the questioners to do their own conjecturing.

Gordo and Manuel came gliding to the street. "Around the corner, *Capitan, si?*" said Gordo. Slade nodded, and the young men set out for the corner at top speed. He hoped they'd catch up with the two devils, but doubted that they would. He pushed his way through the crowd and entered the cantina. Seeing that the table he usually occupied was vacant, he reached it, sat down and rolled a cigarette. Quickly, Carmen and Pablo were with him. The girl's eyes were gerat pools of anxiety. Pablo leaned close, spoke in a low voice—

"Just what did happen? The boys figure it was a ruckus between those two, but I don't think so. What did happen?"

Slade told them, holding nothing back. "Anyhow, I've a notion one of those hellions has a sore arm," he concluded.

Carmen sighed and shook her curly head.

"Why do you have to go thrusting into danger?" Pablo demanded querulously.

"I didn't," Slade denied. "It was waiting for me where I thought I was safe."

"A hairsplitting distinction, I'd say," grunted Pablo. "Well, you're safe in here, at least."

"And here he's going to stay the rest of the night," Carmen declared vigorously. "If he tries to leave, without me, I'll scream my head off."

"I wouldn't want to cause such a commotion," he capitulated. "I'll be good. How about some coffee, and more of Uncle Pablo's pie?"

A little later, Gordo and Manuel strolled in. They shook their heads and rejoined their card game.

"Didn't have any luck, I guess," commented Pablo. "They look real disappointed. They always are when they miss a chance to kill somebody. Have some more pie?"

15

SEVERAL UNEVENTFUL DAYS followed. The valley was peaceful and quiet, the farmers busy, for the season of harvest was drawing near. El Paso experienced a few run-of-mine shootings and cuttings, as was to be expected. Just good clean fun, occasioning little comment. Some brawlers were locked up overnight and released on a promise of good behavior, till the next time.

"Maybe the hellions have decided to pull in their horns," Sheriff Serby remarked hopefully, apropos of the Starlight Riders.

"I don't think so," Slade differed. "That sort don't give up so easily. Some deviltry is cooking, you can rely on it."

Instead of being lulled into a sense of false security by the apparent inactivity of the Starlight Riders, Slade increased his vigilance and left no stone unturned in his efforts to at least alleviate, if not altogether nullify, the fear engendered among the farmers, grape growers and other small owners by their depredations. He took rides up and down the valley, holding converse with the people who lived there.

He was pleased with the change of attitude he found. The farmers and others were stiffening their resistance against the demands of the extortioners. At all times they went armed, and at all times they kept a close watch on their properties. The advent of the tall black-haired man with the cold gray eyes and the quiet, convincing voice replaced fear with confidence. Always his theme was the same—honest men who fought for their lives always came out on top.

"And you've got 'em believing it," chuckled Sheriff Serby.

"It isn't difficult to persuade people to believe the truth, once it is pointed out to them," Slade replied.

"A good deal depends on who's doing the pointing, I'd say," was Serby's dry answer. He chuckled.

"I only hope no harmless cowhands riding to town get blowed from under their hats," he added. "One or two have told me that every time they pass a grape arbor they see a rifle barrel sticking out of it, looking sorta questioning and sorta following their progress till they're outa range."

"All they have to do is keep on riding," Slade smiled reply. "But it wouldn't be advisable to trespass on the farm lands even for an innocent and perfectly legitimate reason."

"They keep on riding, all right," the sheriff grunted. "Say they don't aim to do any riding at all when it's dark. Oh, well, that gives 'em a good excuse to stay overnight in town. A work dodger always figures things to his advantage."

"What we've got to watch out for," Slade continued, "is something big and spectacular, which will again shake people's confidence. And of course the money angle must always be considered, its significance not underestimated."

"How's that?"

"When the money is rolling in, an outlaw leader is sitting pretty," Slade explained. "With plenty of ready cash to spend, his men are contented and have confidence in his leadership. But let the sources of revenue dry up, and his position becomes precarious. He *must* keep his followers' pockets well lined if he hopes to control them. Otherwise they get restless, dissatisfied, and his grip on them loosens. With the result that they are liable to start stupidly operating on their own and bring disaster to the whole outfit. Almost always the head of such a bunch has most of the brains under his hat. Without his direction, the others are likely to go haywire."

"I see," Serby said. Suddenly he shot a direct question at the Ranger: "Walt, have you any notion who's the head of the blasted outfit?"

"Yes, I have," Slade answered. "However, I'm not ready to talk about it, for I could be wrong. I have almost nothing to go on, certainly no proof that I'm right. Deductions based largely on theory can prove to be erroneous."

"You talk like a blasted dictionary, but I reckon I get what you mean," sighed the sheriff. "And I'm ready to bet a hatful of pesos that your deductions, as you call 'em, hit the nail squarely on the head."

"I hope you're right," Slade said. "But there's an old saying, you know, that you've got to catch your rabbit 'fore you cook it, and so far it's a darned elusive rabbit."

"Which will end up with his leg, and all the rest of him, in the trap," Serby predicted confidently.

"Perhaps," Slade conceded. "Anyhow, I think the gentleman is badly in need of a big haul about now. Browse around and see if you can learn something, what would likely be tempting. If we can just manage to forestall what he has in mind, there's a good chance we'll be able to smash the outfit once and for all, and incidentally drop a loop on the big he-wolf of the pack. I doubt if he'd assign such a chore to the hired hands. Would quite likely be present to superintend matters and make sure the job is pulled without a hitch."

"Okay," Serby replied. "I'll rattle my hocks. Here's hoping. Now let's go get something to eat; all this palaver makes me hungry."

As they headed for the restaurant, Slade added, "I'm inclined to think you may be right in your opinion that they're getting pretty well thinned out. Which makes it even more imperative, from their viewpoint, that something big and successful be pulled. Plenty of recruits to be had in the Border country, but gentlemen with share-the-wealth notions don't sign up with a leader who can't produce results.

"And bear in mind," he cautioned, "that we're not up against just a brush-popping bunch of cow thieves, but an outfit as brainy as it is ornery. The other night was a fair example of how they work. I thought I was setting a trap for possibly the head, figuring he might decide to make a try for me himself, seeing as his hands had had no luck. He didn't and set a very nearly successful trap for *me*."

"Just the same, it didn't work," Serby replied cheerfully. "And that's what counts in the long run. In this game there ain't no second best; it's whole hog or nothing. Come along, talking about hogs makes me still hungrier; I hanker for pork chops."

Pork chops for two, plus all the fixin's proved satisfactory on both fronts. After coffee and cigarettes, the sheriff returned to his office. Slade strolled the riverfront for a while, racking his brains in an attempt to anticipate the outlaws' next move. Where they enjoyed an advantage lay in the fact that they *knew* what they intended doing, while he had to guess at it.

Well, he'd outguessed similar outfits; maybe the luck would continue to hold. He paid Shadow a visit but got no encouragement from him. The big black appeared noncommittal as to the future and apparently satisfied with the present.

"You're a big help," Slade told him. "Hope you sit down on a cactus burr."

The outlaws struck!

Struck where Slade and the sheriff least expected them to. Struck expertly and with a daring that verged on impudence.

The bank in El Paso had always been considered safe and

sound, with ample capital, ample surplus, and ample deposits. Its management was in shrewd and conservative hands.

It was also considered safe from physical encroachments. The building which housed it was massive, set on a quiet side street, the two doors adequate. The vault, with its ponderous iron door, appeared to be impervious to anything other than dynamite in large quantities. It wasn't.

The night was very dark, the sky overcast, with only a slight breeze blowing. Dark and still.

The watchman made his round, tried the doors, made sure the window bars were intact. In front of the building he paused, leaning against the trunk of a big tree that grew close to the street, hidden in its shadow. Leaning comfortably against the trunk, he smoked a pipe. He had been doing just that each night for years.

Suddenly he heard a slight rustling amid the leaves above, as if a sleepy bird were changing position. He glanced up idly, an instant too late. From the leafy screen dropped a small loop that settled over his head, around his neck; it was instantly jerked tight, lifting him off his feet. He clawed frantically at the strangling noose, tried to grasp the rope, almost succeeded.

From the tree a man dropped beside him. There was a gleam of steel. The watchman's body jerked spasmodically, shivered from head to foot and then was still, swinging gently in the faint breeze.

The killer, who was masked, stepped away from the tree and beckoned. Three more furtive figures, also masked, stole swiftly across the street to join him. Without a glance for the slain watchman, the murderous quartet hurried to the back door of the building, which of course was locked. One, tall, broad-shouldered, reached for the knob, fumbled a moment. A key clicked softly in the lock, and the door swung open. The four entered, closing and locking the door behind them.

Only a small light burned in the outer room. The vault was in the shadow. The tall man approached and squatted before the door. His companions stationed themselves at the windows, back in the shadow, from where they could view the street.

From a canvas sack he carried, the tall man took a hand drill. He set the steel bit against the door close to the combination knob. The vault, though massive, was old-fashioned and the drill bit swiftly into the fairly soft iron. The low, thin whine of the drill might easily have been mistaken for a rat gnawing the floorboards.

Swiftly and steadily the safecracker worked, drilling one overlapping hole after another. In a surprisingly short time, he drilled out the combination knob. A little more work with the drill, a little with a jimmy, and the door swung open. All four hurried into the vault. The slide of a bull's-eye lantern was cautiously eased back and by its beam the robbers quickly transferred the contents of the vault into stout canvas sacks, leaving only the smaller coins. The tall leader swung the vault door shut against the slight chance it might be noticed from the street. Then the four slipped out the back door, closing and locking it behind them. Less than half an hour had elapsed since the watchman died under the killer's knife.

The bunch reached the street, peered cautiously up and down it, then sped to the mouth of a nearby alley. Another moment and fast hoofs clicked away from town, into the shadowy northwest. Just beyond the outskirts of the town, two drew rein. The other two, with bulging saddle pouches, continued north by slightly east. In front of the bank, the watchman's body swung back and forth in the strengthening wind.

16

HAD NOT THE WIND strengthened appreciably, the robbery and murder might not have been discovered until daybreak. As it was, the wind swung the body into the beam cast by a nearby street light, so that less than two hours had elapsed when a man passing along the street on his way home caught sight of the corpse's grotesque gyrations. He quickened his pace, wondering what the devil it could be. Another moment and he peered close, gave a horrified yell and raced around the corner to the nearest saloon, where he gabbled forth his grisly find.

Men boiled out of the saloon, shouting and cursing. Some ran to the bank, others sped in search of the sheriff and the town marshall.

They found the sheriff in his office, just getting ready to close up shop after a session of book work. He at once accompanied the informants to the bank. The crowd, which had been greatly augmented as the news spread, was milling around the locked doors. Somebody had fetched a lantern, and by its light could be seen the hole in the vault door and the combination knob and drill lying on the floor in front of it.

The sheriff called a couple of men by name. "Go rouse up the cashier—you know where he lives," he ordered. "He'll open the doors. Some of the rest of you locate the marshal and tell him to stick around and keep an eye on things."

He gazed at the hanged body of the watchman and swore bitterly.

"Poor old fellow never had a chance," he growled, and headed for the waterfront.

Walt Slade was sitting at a table with Carmen when the sheriff arrived. He listened to the grim story and nodded.

"Put it over on us neatly," he observed. "Sit down and cool off a bit before you have a stroke or something. I think I know where the devils are headed for, but there's no hurry; we've got a long ride ahead of us. I may be wrong, but I don't believe I am. Too bad about the poor watchman, but this may provide the opportunity we've hoped for. Pablo, bring the sheriff a drink, a couple of them."

Thus admonished, Serby drew up a chair and accepted the drink which he downed at a gulp, taking the second one more slowly. Slade, watching him closely, was gratified that his nerves were steadying; Sheriff Serby wasn't as young as he'd once been.

"Okay," Slade said at length, "let's go. The bank first." He reached over and patted Carmen's shoulder and smiled.

"Be seeing you soon," he promised.

Carmen watched his tall form out the door. "Uncle Pablo," she said slowly, "I don't think I could take it for a lifetime."

When Slade and the sheriff reached the bank, they found that the cashier had arrived before them, and so had the town marshal and a couple of Serby's deputies.

"Tell one of them to round up the other deputy and meet us at the office," Slade told Serby in low tones. "Tell them to have the rigs on their horses; we'll be riding very shortly."

They entered the bank, where the cashier was endeavoring to check the rifled vault.

"Any notion how much they got, Herb?" the sheriff asked.

"I can't say for sure," replied the cashier, "but it was plenty. More than fifty thousand at the least."

Slade was examining the damaged vault door. "Fellow knew his business," he remarked. "Those holes are drilled with micrometer precision. Don't often run across that sort in this section."

"How the devil did they get into the building?" the cashier wondered. "The locks weren't forced."

"Managed to get a wax impress and make a key," Slade replied. "No chore for such an expert as the hellion who opened the vault must be."

He did not mention that in his opinion, the gentleman in question was thoroughly familiar with the layout of the building and doubtless had access to the offices in the back, which he had been able to visit without attracting any attention.

"Let's go," he told Serby. "Nothing more we can do here." He gazed at the body of the murdered watchman for an instant, his face set in granite lines, his eyes cold as frosted steel. "Let's go," he repeated.

"First, though," he added abruptly, "let's try and find where they left their horses while doing the chore; should be close."

"There's an alley right around the corner," said Serby.

"Very likely that's it," Slade replied. "Let's investigate. Bring a lantern."

It took the Ranger but a few minutes to locate the spot where the horses had been tethered to a convenient rail. He examined the ground closely, studied the hoofprints in the soft earth.

"Four horses stood here," he announced. "That will be the number of those who took part in the robbery, four. Evidently the cream of the bunch; they certainly knew their business. Okay, let's head for the office."

When they reached the office, they found the three deputies already there.

"The five of us should be enough," Slade decided. In a few terse sentences he outlined his experience with the old trail and the cabin in the clearing, for the deputies', benefit.

"I may be wrong, but I think that's where they're headed for," he concluded. "Anyhow, we'll try and find out for sure."

He and the sheriff quickly secured their mounts. Twenty minutes later they were riding north by slightly east.

With the plainsman's unerring instinct for distance and direction, Slade had no difficulty locating the beginning of the old trail, despite the handicap of darkness.

"Would be to our advantage to get there before daylight, but I doubt if we can," he said as the horses toiled upward. "We mustn't make any slips, for it's a desperate bunch, and I don't think they'll be taken without a fight."

"We'll take 'em one way or the other," growled the sheriff. "I'm itching to line sights with those snake-blooded skunks."

"Keep your eyes and ears open," Slade admonished the others. "There's just the chance that they might head back this way, although I really don't think so. Best not to take chances."

"I reckon you'll hear 'em long before they hear us, if they do head back this way," said Serby. "Blazes, it's dark!"

It was dark, black dark, but Slade knew the way was open and let Shadow set the pace. He carefully estimated the distance covered, checking it against his recollection of how far it was to the cabin in the clearing. He felt fairly confident that he could locate the spot and not overshoot it. Besides, there would undoubtedly be some light before so very long.

There was, a faint graying in the east. The dawn was heralded by the chirping of birds, quickly increasing in volume and now accompanied by bursts of song. Slade slowed the pace; he knew they were no great distance from their goal, and he still kept in mind the possibility of the outlaws, or some of them, heading back to town with the advent of daybreak.

However, the trail wound on, silent and deserted, still shadowy under the growth. He began searching with his eyes for certain landmarks he had subconsciously implanted in his memory. With a sense of satisfaction he recognized several by which to steer his course.

The light was growing stronger. Slade slowed the horses again, to a walk. His companions, realizing they were nearing their objectives, tensed for instant action. A glance at the grim faces relieved Slade of any anxiety as to the outcome. All four were men of good courage and intelligence, and all four were excellent shots.

Four in the outlaw band, at least, for there was no guarantee that others of the bunch had not been waiting in the cabin. Well, they'd have to take their chance on that. Slade counted on the element of surprise to be in their favor. He wished it were darker, but they'd have to make the best of it. He considered the location of the cabin, its door fronting the brush where they'd hole up, also in their favor. Was but a few yards from the brush to the door; they might well catch the devils settin'.

A little later, he distinctly smelled smoke. "They're in there," he breathed. "And here's where we turn the cayuses into the brush and leave them. Tie yours to branches—Shadow will stand. And hope they don't take a notion to sing songs to the morning star. If they do, the hellions will be on the *qui vive,* and we'll likely get a reception we won't like."

With the horses concealed in the brush, they wormed their way to the clearing. Through the leafy screen of the final straggle, Slade studied the building; it showed no signs of occupancy other than the trickle of smoke rising from the chimney. The lean-to was still in the shadow, and he could not tell for sure just how many horses were tethered there. He thought he could make out two, but beyond their position the gloom was thick.

"All set?" he whispered. "Make straight for the door. I'll hit it with my shoulder—it won't be locked. Then right in and ready for business; don't take chances."

A moment more and the posse charged across the clearing, Slade in the lead. He hit the door with his shoulder, all his muscular two hundred pounds behind it. The door flew open, and they were in the cabin.

Two men sitting at a table with cups of coffee in front of them leaped to their feet, jerking their guns. Slade fired with both hands, seeking to cripple rather than kill, for the instant his eyes rested on the pair he earnestly desired to take at least one of them alive.

But his companions were not governed by such considerations; they shot to kill. Back and forth gushed the orange flashes. The cabin rocked to the boom of the guns. A moment later Slade lowered his guns and gazed through the smoke mist at the two forms sprawled on the floor. Yes, his companions had shot to kill; the outlaws were riddled with bullets.

Slade regarded them in bitter disappointment; he felt that once more he had been neatly outsmarted. How? He hadn't the least notion. But instead of four robbers holed up in the cabin, there had been but two, and neither was the man or men he had earnestly hoped to kill or capture.

The cabin showed indications of occupancy for a considerable length of time. There were stores of staple provisions stacked on shelves, tumbled blankets on bunks built against the wall, hooks and gratings in the stone-lined fireplace. Several rifles stood in a corner. There were chairs and the table, homemade but of good construction. Doubtless the original occupant had left the furnishings intact when he moved away or died.

Sheriff Serby also gazed—glared, rather—at the slain outlaws and rubbed his hands together with grim satisfaction.

"But where in blazes is the money?" he demanded. "I don't see it anywhere."

"We'll find it, if it's here," said Slade. "I'm beginning to get a notion as to where it is."

"Now I reckon we'll just sit tight and wait for the others to come back, eh?" Serby asked.

"Maybe," Slade replied. "Come along Trevis, I want to have a look at those horses under the lean-to."

Under the lean-to were only two horses, one divested of its rig, the other with only the bit flipped so the animal could eat in comfort, its saddle pouches well plumped out. Slade unbuckled one and thrust his hand inside, bringing out packets of bills and rolls of coin.

"Here's the bank money," he said. "I've a notion all of it is here."

The sheriff swore exultantly. "Not a bad night, after all," he congratulated. "How in blazes did you figure it would be where it is?"

"Played a hunch, in a fashion," Slade answered. He gazed at the horses.

"Trevis," he said, "we might as well head back to town with

the dinero and the bodies. The others are not returning. Not tonight, and I doubt if ever."

"What makes you think that?" asked the bewildered peace officer.

"Because of the condition of these horses," Slade replied. "One was all set to travel after it finished its meal. One of the robbers planned to ride to town with the money and deliver it to the head of the outfit, which he could safely do in broad daylight. Then the others would visit the head, one at a time, and receive their divvy. Last night the four split up after robbing the bank. Two came straight to the cabin by way of what they considered a trail never used. The other two returned to El Paso."

"But why didn't they take the money with them?" Serby asked, his bewilderment increasing.

"Because," Slade explained, "they were not sure but that the robbery and murder would be discovered sooner than they hoped, as it was. They knew that anybody riding into town might well be intercepted and questioned and took no chances, as they would have been taking were they packing the money along. Shrewd and farseeing. Were they stopped, they would doubtless have advanced a perfectly legitimate reason for being out together at that time of night. A pair with brains."

What he did not mention was the fact that being convinced in his own mind as to the identity of the pair substantiated his deductions.

The sheriff swore some more. "The way you figure things out is plumb beyond me," he complained. "But when you lay it before me, it's plain to see as a cowpoke in church. How in blazes do you do it?"

Slade smiled and changed the subject.

"There'll be some very angry gentlemen in El Paso tomorrow," he predicted. "I venture to say this is the last thing they expected to happen. Yes, at last I'm ready to agree with you that we've got them on the run. They've very likely to do something foolish before long and give us the opportunity we hope for. I thought we had it tonight, but it didn't work out just as expected. As usual, the hellions were a jump ahead of me."

"Can't agree to that," protested Serby. "How could you be expected to know they figured to split up like they did? You can see into the trunk of a tree farther than most, but there's a limit for even you."

"That was definitely proved," Slade laughed. "Let's go."

When they arrived at the cabin, one of the deputies had a big boiler of coffee on the make.

"Plenty of bacon and eggs, too, and some tinned sausages and a slab of cake," he announced. "Figured we might as well put away a surroundin' while we're waiting. We shoved the carcasses over to one side so nobody'll trip over 'em and get hurt. And one of us can keep watch while the others eat."

"Fine!" Slade said. "I'm feeling a mite lank, and I reckon the rest of you are, too. Been a busy night. Nobody needs to stand watch. We won't be interrupted."

"If you say so, guess it is," the deputy conceded cheerfully. "Be comin' up in ten minutes. Pete, rustle some of those tin plates and cups and knives and forks. Sorry I ain't got napkins and a tablecloth, gents, but I reckon we'll make out."

They did, sleeves, when necessary, serving as a workable substitute for napkins.

17

AFTER EATING, they took time out for a smoke. Then they roped the bodies to the horses, and the grim cavalcade set out for town.

Progress with the laden horses was slow, and they reached El Paso in the middle of the afternoon. After caring for their mounts, Slade and Serby repaired to the bank with the money pouches which they delivered to the astounded officials.

The cashier made a quick check of the pouches' contents. "So far as I can see, there's not a peso missing," he announced. "There'll be a nice reward for you fellows, Mr. Slade."

"I suggest," Slade said gently, "that if your watchman left any dependents, it would be a good idea to hand it to them."

The banker regarded the tall Ranger with respect. "Just as you say, Mr. Slade," he acceded. "I doubt if anybody will argue the point."

"I'd like to see 'em try it," growled Serby. "Come on, Walt, I've about finished with the bacon and eggs, and I crave nourishment."

As they left the bank, Slade observed, "Mind if we eat at Pablo's place? He'll want to know what happened."

"And the little gal will want to see you back in one piece," said the sheriff. "Let's go!"

Pablo was glad to hear what happened, and Carmen more than glad to see Slade back safe and sound.

"You'd drive any woman crazy," she declared, after the tale was finished.

"Isn't the first time you've said that," he reminded her. Carmen blushed.

After enjoying a really excellent meal, quite an improvement over their sketchy breakfast, Sheriff Serby stifled a yawn.

"And now," he 'lowed, "I crave some shuteye."

"Me too," Slade agreed.

"Makes three of us," said Carmen. "Of course I didn't go to bed last night. How could I? As I told you before, you'll be the death of me yet."

"But what a way to die!" he chuckled.

"Shut up!" she retorted. "You're impossible."

Slade and the sheriff were showered with congratulations, for Serby absolutely refused to take the credit for the killing of the two robbers and the recovery of the bank money.

"Darndest best deputy he ever had," was avowed in many quarters, it being assumed that the sheriff had appointed Slade a deputy.

Serby did nothing to correct the misconception. "I don't see how it can do any harm, and it may do some good," he insisted. "The El Halcon yarn is just about forgot."

"Not in certain quarters, I fear," Slade replied. "Well, I hope it isn't. I hope the hellions keep on thinking I'm just another owlhoot who figures to run them out and take over their good thing. Such things have happened, you know, and their sort are always ready to believe the worst of anybody. Let them keep on thinking so and tip their hand."

"And you don't think they've spotted you for a Ranger?"

"No, I don't" Slade answered. "I could be wrong, but I don't think I am. I certainly hope not. Otherwise I'm afraid they might cover up or even pull out altogether. But so far as I know, there are but a few people here who know the truth. You and the commissioners, of course, and Pablo and Carmen. And I have every faith in all of you keeping a tight latigo on your jaws."

Despite the congratulations, which were pleasant to receive, El Halcon was far from satisfied with the way things were going. He had, with the help of others, managed to do away with quite a few of the "hired hands," but the brains of the outfit were still at large, and he could hope for no real lasting peace until they were done away with or apprehended. And already innocent men had died. He earnestly hoped that at least there would be no more killings.

"I still think the money problem may well prove to be the crux of the situation," he observed to the sheriff. "The head must be getting a bit frantic. Been quite a while since he made a really good haul. Twice, now, he figured he had one in the bag—the train wreck and the bank robbery—but it turned out he didn't. I think what followers he has left may be getting a bit unruly. Their sort shy away from failure, and of late he's been failing with regularity. There's a limit to how much they'll take. If the bank robbery had been successful to the extent of tieing onto the money, his grip on them would have been firm again. But the way it turned out, with the money recovered and two of the bunch done in, I wouldn't be surprised if they're sort of looking sideways at him."

"Maybe one of 'em will do the job for us," the sheriff remarked hopefully.

"Not likely," Slade replied. "They're more apt to just show up missing some morning. Having departed for new and greener pastures. But a leader of his ability can, sooner or later, always get more. Until he is disposed of, and his very able assistant also, he still poses a threat that cannot be ignored. Brains, courage and utter ruthlessness make a formidable combination, and he has all three."

A silence followed, each busy with his own thoughts as they smoked and gazed out of the window with eyes that were really focused elsewhere. Finally Serby spoke, shifting his gaze back to the Ranger's face.

"Walt," he said, "do you really figure you know who the head of the bunch is?"

"I do," Slade replied. "There is no doubt in my mind as to who is the leader of the Starlight Riders."

"But you're not ready to talk about it?"

Slade hesitated a moment, arrived at a decision.

"Yes, I am," he said. "It may give you something of a start, but I think it is time you knew. The leader of the Starlight Riders is Bruce Parker, the supposed-to-be promoter and real estate man, ably assisted by Clay Regan, owner of the Full-House saloon, supposedly wrecked by the Starlight Riders because Regan refused to pay tribute for so-called protection."

Serby started and blinked. "You don't mean it!" he exclaimed.

"I do," Slade repeated.

"But—but—" sputtered the bewildered peace officer.

"I'll start at the beginning, which was the train wreck, where I got my first lead, although I didn't recognize it as such at the time. Remember that talkative passenger who told us he recalled seeing two of the train wreckers in the Full-House the night there was a ruckus in the place? Well, what he told us interested me in the Full-House. What he had to say appeared to corroborate what you told me about the trouble in the place, that Regan had knuckled under to the bunch after a little demonstration of what they would do to anybody who opposed them.

"Okay. I made it my business to drop in at the Full-House to have a look at the place and its owner. Another little happening that night that I'll come to later. Well, I studied Regan a bit, and he certainly did not strike me as a man who would knuckle under to anybody. There is no such thing as a criminal physiognomy, as I've mentioned to you before. Were there, the work of the law enforcement officer would be much simplified. But there are certain facial structures from which a man's disposition and character can be fairly well judged. Regan has all the earmarks of a fighter and a salty hombre, which he is."

"I'll agree with you there," the sheriff nodded.

"Well," Slade continued, "While I was there I got to talking with a waiter, a harmless individual who has no connections with the Riders, who replaced the man Regan had fired a few days before. He described the fight that took place there. I instantly knew that the fight was a phony, deliberately staged for some reason. A spectacular throwing of chairs, overturning of tables, a lot of yelling and breaking of bottles and chair legs, no real damage done. A few wild shots were fired, and it was claimed that a bartender had his hand grazed by a slug, as to that I don't know, but I doubt it. Yes, the fight, so called, was deliberately staged."

"But why?" asked the sheriff.

"As a cover-up," Slade explained. "Perhaps Regan figured that somebody, for some reason, was getting suspicious of him. So he, or the head, put on that really quite clever little act. Everybody, including yourself, at once jumped to the conclusion that Regan had been approached by the Starlight Riders, had resisted their demands and then had come across to them after a little demonstration of what they were capable of doing to stubborn customers. The word was skillfully spread around, and everybody believed it.

"I got to thinking rather seriously of Regan, figuring him to be connected with the Riders, perhaps their head, although he did not strike me as an individual capable of as subtle and carefully planned and functioned a scheme as the extortion. He is more the stage robber and cattle rustler type."

Again the sheriff nodded agreement. Slade rolled and lighted a cigarette and resumed—

"Then the body of Regan's former waiter, the supposed-to-be chuck-line-riding cowhand who turned his hand to waiting on tables, was picked up in the brush the other side of Clint. The man I felt certain had been killed by the Starlight Riders. Just why I don't know, nor is it important. I'd say he either welshed, tried his hand at a little blackmail, or got cold feet. That strengthened the case against Regan, although by that time I'd begun to wonder a little about somebody else."

"How's that?" asked Serby.

"Remember when Parker came over to our table in the Texas Street place? Well, I knew at once that he came to get a good look at me. He tried to conceal his intention, but his eyes showed it. He had heard of how the express car robbery was frustrated. I'm of the opinion that he knew me to be El Halcon. I didn't think anything of it at the time. But now is where the element of chance enters the picture, the unexplainable something that makes one wonder. Just before I entered the Full-House that night, Parker came out. He glanced about. I knew he saw me, but he pretended not to and hurried off. A rather unusual procedure, don't you think? When one runs into an acquaintance, especially in such a locality, one naturally reacts to the extent of a nod, a word or the wave of a hand. I thought Parker's reaction was peculiar. He slipped a mite, shrewd as he is, in pretending not to see me. Why? I didn't know, but it caused me to wonder a mite. Of course he had gone to the Full-House for a conference with Regan, his partner and assistant in the Starlight Rider business. And to warn him that El Halcon, the owlhoot with a reputation for horning in on the good things other folks have started, was in the section and already in action.

"Then, very shortly afterward, the very nearly successful attempt on my life was made.

"But of course, although I was wondering a little about Parker and his peculiar actions, I wasn't giving him any really serious thought; I was beginning to concentrate on Regan. Now we'll go back to the train wreck and my first real lead, so far as Parker was concerned. You will recall the slip of paper you hauled out of one of the dead wrecker's pockets. I knew at once that that plat of the railroad between El Paso and Ysleta was drawn by an engineer, or at least a surveyor." The sheriff nodded, his interest growing.

"So again the element of chance," Slade continued. "I happened to stroll down into the Chamizal Zone, and there I ran into Bruce Parker supposedly laying out a site for one of the hotels he'd let it be known he intended to erect. A surveyor was running lines and taking measurements. He made a slight slip, which Parker instantly detected. Parker took over the transit and showed himself perfectly familiar with the instrument and the principles of surveying. I sincerely doubted that there were two men in the section with the knowledge required to draw that plat of the railroad and accurately note the point where the train was to be wrecked, and do it in a manner that would be plain to those entrusted with the chore of wrecking and robbery. So at once, with everything else considered, I felt sure Parker was my man. His promoting and his real estate operations provided a perfect cover-up."

The sheriff shook his head in wordless admiration. "You sure make out a case against him," he said.

"Yes," Slade replied, "but, unfortunately, one that would not stand up in court. Here's a final angle that I consider the clincher of the circumstantial case against Parker. I feel that I am safe in assuming that he's pretty well thought of at the bank."

"That's right," acceded Serby. "He's a good depositor, and he has made some pretty shrewd real estate deals and has gotten them to take a more than mild interest in his promotion notions, with which he would of course need banking help."

"And has entrance to the offices in the back of the building," Slade pointed out, "giving him a chance to familiarize himself with the layout and an opportunity to obtain the wax impress from which he made the key that quietly opened the back door of the building."

"Darned if that don't sound reasonable," conceded the sheriff.

"Yes, another link in the chain, but still nothing from which we could make a court case. A good lawyer would tear the whole structure to pieces in no time. We still have to get something definite on the hellion."

"You'll get it, no doubt in my mind as to that," the old peace officer declared.

"Hope you're right."

"Was I ever wrong?" sighed Serby. "Let's go eat."

18

Once again Sheriff Serby understood why Slade was considered not only the most daring but the ablest of the Texas Rangers. It was not his physical prowess and his extraordinary speed and accuracy with a gun, but his keen mind that placed him in the forefront of the illustrious body of law enforcement officers.

Walt Slade not only outshot the owlhoots, he out-thought them.

At the restaurant they occupied a secluded table, where they could talk. A waiter took their orders and departed.

"Think the hellions will ever use that old cabin again?" Serby asked.

"On the face of it, one would deem it unlikely," Slade replied. "But it is not wise to put too much dependence on the obvious. Under certain circumstances it might prove to their advantage to do so, even though we know its location and how to get there. Something to keep in mind."

"Yes, the hellions are all the time doing what we least expect," the sheriff conceded gloomily.

"Like the bank job," Slade said. "They put that one over on us very neatly."

"And if it hadn't been for you prowling around and finding that old trail, they would have put it over one hundred percent," replied Serby. "Mighty smart thinking on your part."

"Experience, rather," Slade differed. "As I have remarked, outlaw methods and procedure usually fall into a definite pattern. To an extent from necessity. A bunch can't go riding out of town together on a marauding expedition without running the risk of attracting attention. Whereas leaving one at a time to gather at a prearranged rendezvous occasions no comment. So a hangout somewhere in the hills or other wastelands is essential. I worked on that premise, knowing that if there was a hangout there must be a way to reach it, a way not generally known and infrequently traveled."

For some time the sheriff addressed himself to his food, then suddenly he asked, "And you figure it was Parker who arranged that straw dummy and the try at drygulching from the alley?"

"Oh, I suppose Regan and the two horned toads assigned to the chore did the actual work of arranging the dummy and setting it out for bait, but it was Parker who told them what to do and how to do it. While I was sitting in the Full-House, I saw Regan cock his ear as if listening to something. Then he slipped into the back room and shut the door behind him. I didn't think anything of it at the time, figuring he'd probably been called to the back room by a swamper or somebody to check stock for the bar, or something. Later, however, it occurred to me that Parker must have circled around, entered the saloon by the back door and called to Regan. I figure he told him El Halcon would have to be eliminated pronto."

"And set the trap?"

"That's right. And it might have worked if they hadn't overlooked one small detail and left the dummy's leg bent forward at the knee joint instead of backward or straight out."

"I'll never get over how you spotted that one," chuckled Serby. "Something nobody else would have noticed."

"Experience again," Slade smiled. "There's an old saying, 'Look before you leap.' The 'book' of the Rangers says look twice, then don't jump—walk, slowly; you may have missed something. Let's have some more coffee."

After the coffee and a cigarette, Serby returned to his office. Slade strolled about town, pondering the problem that still confronted him, the problem that for a brief period he had thought was solved. He had been confident that the raid on the cabin hangout would be the finish of the bunch.

However, things had not worked out in that convenient fashion. Once again he felt that he had been outsmarted, and El Halcon didn't take kindly to being outsmarted. He had thought to catch the two chief malefactors red-handed, as the saying went, with their only choice between death and surrendering to justice. He had failed in his objective. The slaying of the two members of the band and the recovery of the stolen money represented but a partial victory, the winning of a skirmish, as it were, with the main battle postponed, perhaps indefinitely. For now the two devils would undoubtedly be very cautious, might even refrain from action of any kind for a while, till things cooled down a bit.

Well, all he could do was resolve himself to patience. Perhaps circumstances he didn't know about would force them into impetuous action. What? Once again he had not the slightest notion. But perhaps he'd get a break.

He continued his slow stroll, still pondering the situation as it stood and getting exactly nowhere. Turning a corner, he passed Bruce Parker's office, the location of which Sheriff Serby had mentioned. The door was shut, and a glance through the window showed a single room untenanted. Slade hesitated a moment, then turned his steps toward the Chamizal Zone and the proposed site of the hotel Parker claimed he intended to build. The site was deserted, with no indications of any work having been done, which was what he expected, although he thought it possible that Parker might be fooling around there for the benefit of possible observers of his activities.

Once again Slade hesitated, debating what would be his next move. Sunset was thundering its chromatic splendor in the west, and El Paso's nocturnal denizens were beginning to stir. He headed for the Full-House. The rush would not start for a little while, but the place should already be filling up.

It was. There were quite a few cowhands and rivermen at the bar, a couple of games going, one roulette wheel spinning. Slade sat down at a table and gave his order to the pleasant and talkative waiter who had served him twice before. The waiter volunteered some news.

"Boss won't be in tonight," he remarked. "Took a little trip over east somewhere; left on the eleven A.M. train. Didn't say when he'd be back, but I figure he won't be gone long, not more than a day or two."

Slade sipped his drink and endeavored to digest this bit of information. He wondered if there was any significance attached to it. Probably not. Regan might have any number of reasons for taking a short trip—a business matter, a visit with friends or relatives. But any move on the part of the saloonkeeper or Bruce Parker was of interest to El Halcon.

The Full-House did not appear productive of results. Slade lingered a while, then went in search of Sheriff Serby, whom he finally located at the Texas Street restaurant, having a bite to eat.

"See anything of Parker today?" Slade asked as he dropped into a chair.

"Saw him in the bank early this morning, talking with the cashier," Serby replied. "Why?"

"Frankly, I don't know," Slade replied. "He wasn't in his office when I passed by, and he wasn't at the supposed-to-be site of his riverfront hotel, and Clay Regan left town on the late morning train, heading east. I was just wondering if there was any connection."

Serby laid down his knife and fork. "Think they might be planning to pull out?" he asked.

"I don't think so, at least not just yet," Slade answered, adding grimly, "but they might be planning something we will hear about, sooner or later."

They most certainly would.

The Sunrise Limited pulled out of Marfa late. Bouncing around on his seatbox, old Ad Cardigan, the engineer, was getting all he could out of his big locomotive, for he hoped to make up some of the lost time in the course of the hundred mile run to Sierra Blanca. He widened the throttle a little, hooked up his reverse lever another notch on the quadrant. He glanced at the steam gage needle quivering against the two-hundred-pounds pressure mark and opened the injector a trifle, sending a larger stream of water pouring into the straining boiler.

The fireman also glanced at the needle, hopped down from his seatbox. A hot glare filled the cab as he swung open the fire door, and the musical clatter and clang of a shovel bailing coal into the roaring furnace. He slammed the door shut, resumed his seat and peered out the window. The headlight beam glittered on the twin steel ribbons unrolling on and on before the spinning wheels.

Back in the coaches, the passengers relaxed in drowsy comfort. Everything was peaceful on the Sunrise Limited, or so it seemed.

In the express car, the messenger sat working at his little desk. He did not hear the supposedly locked rear door open. It was locked, all right, but any lock responds to the turning of a key, legitimate or otherwise.

Through the opening glided two masked men, tall, powerfully built men, carrying guns in their hands. The first intimation the messenger had of their presence was a tap on his shoulder. He jerked around to stare into the black gun muzzles.

"All right," said the foremost gunman, in a deep, growling and evidently disguised voice. "All right, open that safe and be quick about it."

Facing the threat of the two guns, there was nothing the messenger could do but obey. With shaking hands he twirled the combination knob till the tumblers clicked and the massive door swung open.

"Now the inner compartment door," said the gunman, who was evidently thoroughly familiar with the layout of a safe.

The messenger unlocked it. The instant he did so, a gun

barrel crashed against his skull and he fell senseless to the floor.

The two robbers quickly transferred the contents of the safe to a canvas bag one carried. Then they turned and sped to the rear door of the car, first glancing through the window. The train was traveling a straight stretch of track that extended for some distance. On either side of the right of way were low, brush-grown rises, from the crests of which the railroad was in plain view.

In the engine cab the air whistle let out a shrill screech, and kept on screeching. Somewhere back in the train somebody was pulling a cord.

Cardigan swore an exasperated oath. There went the time he'd hoped to make up! "What the devil!" He snorted, slammed the throttle shut and applied the air. The brake shoes ground against the wheels, the Sunrise came to a jolting stop. Cardigan leaned out the window, glaring back along the halted train.

A lantern bobbed into view. The blue-coated conductor came trotting toward the engine.

"What's the matter?" he shouted.

"How the blankety-blank-blank would I know?" Cardigan bawled back. "Somebody pulled the whistle cord on me."

"Well, I didn't," the conductor denied. "There's nothing wrong back here; get going!"

In the confusion, nobody saw the two robbers slip from between the express car and the following coach and fade into the brush that lined the right of way.

Cardigan watched until he saw the lantern wave a highball, then, still swearing, continued on his belated way.

As the train roared away, two riders emerged from the brush not far off, leading two saddled and bridled horses. The two robbers appeared from the growth. A few muttered words and they mounted the led horses and the four headed for Marfa at a fast pace.

Nobody paid any attention to the two passengers who boarded the eastbound at Marfa. Nobody paid any attention to them when they left the train at Sanderson and were lost in the crowd that swarmed the main street in the shadow of a canyon wall.

Not until the Sunrise reached Sierra Blanca, where the express was due to be unloaded, was the robbery discovered, the still-unconscious messenger lying in front of the rifled safe, his head in a pool of blood that had flowed from his split scalp.

19

WORD WAS CLICKED over the wires in every direction, warning sheriffs and other peace officers to be on the look-out for the robbers. The trouble was, nobody knew where in Hades to look.

A wire to Sheriff Serby requested that a doctor meet the Sunrise at El Paso, to care for the injured messenger. Serby dispatched a deputy to fetch a doctor and hurried to locate Walt Slade, whom he found at Pablo's.

"We'll meet the train, it should be here any minute," Slade said.

The headlight of the Sunrise was blazing into view when they reached the station. A moment later the train ground to a halt.

The messenger had recovered consciousness but could add little to what was already known except numbering the robbers as two.

"How much did they get?" the sheriff asked.

"There was ten thousand dollars in the safe, consigned to the El Paso bank," the messenger replied as the doctor treated his injury. "Should be somebody here from the bank to receive their consignment."

There was, but he didn't receive any money.

"Well, they put that one over nicely," Slade remarked as he and the sheriff walked back to Pablo's.

"You figure it was Parker and Regan?"

"Of course," Slade replied. "All the earmarks of the way they'd pull a job. Unfortunately, though, no matter how convinced we may be in our own minds, there is not one iota of proof against them. I wouldn't be surprised if Parker somehow managed to learn from somebody at the bank that the money would be on the Sunrise."

"Think we ought to speak to the bankers?" Serby asked. Slade shook his head.

"Would do us no good, and somebody might do some loose talking that would do harm," the Ranger disagreed. "If somebody at the bank did let that bit of information slip, it is logical to believe he'd be reluctant to admit it. Besides, it wouldn't mean anything, anyhow. It would just confirm my belief that Parker and Regan were the robbers, and I don't need any confirmation. Oh, they worked it smoothly, all right. They didn't leave El Paso together, of course. I imagine they boarded the Sunrise at Sanderson. Nobody would have paid them any mind. And I'll wager they are not seen here until a a couple of days have passed, and they'll have a plausible explanation for their absence, if one is requested. Well, now the devil is well heeled and fixed to set up in business again. If he needs more men, he can get them, with ten thousand dollars in his kitty. So our troubles start all over."

"Well, anyhow, I'm in the clear so far as this one is concerned," said the sheriff. "It didn't happen in my county."

"But I'm not in the clear," Slade returned morosely. "It happened in Texas, and Texas is my 'county.' Rattle your hocks, I feel the need of a drink, and some coffee to hold it down.

"Oh, well," he added cheerfully, "as the poet said, in every life some rain must fall; maybe the sun will shine tomorrow."

"I'd sure like to cloud up and rain a shower of forty-five slugs on those two hellions," the sheriff growled. "Then the sun will really shine for me. Here we are. Now for that snort."

The snort helped. So did the coffee, steaming hot. And Carmen's smile helped even more. Very quickly Slade was back to his normal optimistic self. The pistol-whipped messenger was not seriously injured, so at least the devils didn't kill anybody. Which also helped.

Slade's estimate of when Parker and Regan would show up in El Paso proved accurate. Two days passed before they put in an appearance, and they didn't arrive on the same train. If they offered any explanation for their absence, which they were certainly not required to do, he didn't hear about it Nor did he try to find out, for he was not much interested.

In fact, he considered the train robbery of minor importance. What he really desired to pin on the two devils were the murders of the bank watchman and the farmers. That was what really counted. And he was determined to do it.

Later, when he contacted Sheriff Serby, he found that law enforcement officer in a bad temper.

"I met that blankety-blank Parker in the Texas Street place," he explained. "And I got the feeling he was laughing up his sleeve at me; looked as smug as a cat full of cream and canary."

"Hope you didn't show your feelings," Slade said.

"I didn't," Serby assured him, "but I darn nigh busted a cinch keeping it bottled up."

Slade believed him. As a rule, the sheriff's face was as impassive as a deal board.

"The blankety-blank will laugh on the other side of his face before things are finished," Serby predicted in a growling voice. Slade hoped he was right.

"At least we have one thing to be thankful for—they didn't make a really big haul," he remarked. "Ten thousand dollars is a lot of money, but not so much when it's divided up between half a dozen or more, the way that sort usually drink and gamble and hand it over to women. Doesn't take long to get rid of a sizeable sum. And that's one drawback to easy money, even if it happens to come honestly—the sense of proportion is lost and, before he knows it, the recipient is quite likely to find himself in straitened circumstances financially, with the urge to try and tie onto more of the same kind, which is liable not to be simple. Even honest easy money had been known to start a man riding a crooked trail."

Sheriff Serby nodded soberly. That had been his experience in his long career as a law enforcement officer.

"Yes, I've seen more than one fine young feller make a big killing at cards or dice and go plumb loco," he said. "Within a month or so flat busted and in trouble. There just ain't no such thing as easy money.

"Which certain gents with El Halcon on their trail are going to find out," he concluded with grim confidence.

A little later he added, "Railroad detectives, as they call themselves, though my experience has been that they do darn little detectin', questioned the express messenger. They were wondering if he had forgotten to lock the rear door of the car. He swore up and down that the door was locked, the key in his desk, and the conductor's duplicate was never out of his possession."

"That was an angle I felt verified my conclusion that Parker pulled the job," Slade answered. "At the bank, he proved himself to be an able safe cracker and locksmith, something you don't often run across in this section. Usually, when a safe is opened here, it is done with a sledge hammer and dynamite or nitro. A little item like a locked door wouldn't bother him."

"Evidently it didn't," the sheriff agreed dryly. "If we ever get him behind bars, I'll use spikes and a log chain on him, and weld it."

Slade chuckled. "So before long, our horned toads will have to get busy again," he summed up. "Perhaps the success of their last venture will make them overconfident, and we may get the jump on them."

In which there was a grain of comfort, but not a large enough grain to satisfy El Halcon, or even render him complacent.

The big, so far unanswered, question was: where would the outlaws strike? Twice, Slade felt, he had been thoroughly outsmarted, especially where the bank job was concerned. The hellions were certainly not lacking in brains, daring and initiative. Bruce Parker was proving to be a formidable opponent for even El Halcon. Well, he had confronted formidable opponents before and had eventually outsmarted them. So he did not lack precedent with which to bolster his confidence.

"Let's go eat," suggested the sheriff. "Maybe we'll get a break."

They got the break, in a most unexpected manner. A grizzled old rancher rode into town and visited the sheriff's office.

"Hello, Branch," the sheriff greeted. "What brings a spavined old coot like you to town? The barkeeps won't serve you, they won't let you in a game, and the girls won't waste a look on you."

" 'Pears, from what I see in front of me, they 'low most anything to run loose in this loco town," retorted the oldster. "Oh, well, takes all kinds of folks to make Texas. Reckon even the lowliest critters must have their uses, otherwise the Good Lord wouldn't have made 'em. Fellers like you, the frazzled end of a misspent life, are a sorta warnin' to the rest of us to live better."

Having mutually affronted each other, the two oldsters got down to business. First Serby introduced the cattleman to Slade.

"This is Branch Cooley, Walt," he said. "He owns a spread down toward the south end of the valley; farmers ain't crowded him out yet. Branch, know Walt Slade, an *amigo* of mine."

Cooley shook hands and his shrewd old eyes looked the Ranger up and down.

"Seems I've sorta heard of you, Mr. Slade," he said. "You're the young feller who lent the Otey boys a hand the night those hellions tried to burn 'em out, ain't you?"

"That's right," put in the sheriff. "He's a right hombre."

"So I gather," agreed Cooley. "What brought me to town? I'll tell you, Trev. May sound sorta silly, but it's got me worried a mite, the way things have been going hereabouts of late. Yep, I own a spread, Mr. Slade, the Flying Diamond. Ain't a very big one, but a good one, and I got good stock."

"I think I noticed some of your cows the day I rode into the valley," Slade interpolated. "I thought them excellent in appearance. Don't recall spotting your house though."

"Can't see it from the trail," Cooley replied. "Sets back and behind a grove. Well, as I was sayin', I got good stock, and we've been getting a shipping herd together—will be ready to roll in a couple of days. Back in the old days, when I was a young feller, I was one of Wallace's scouts, and I learned to use my eyes and read the woods and the hills. For the past few days, now, there's been a feller ridin' up in the hills, who I'm pretty sure is keeping tabs on what we're doing. He tries to keep out of sight and does a pretty good chore of it, but I spotted him three times, shadowin' along through the brush. Didn't think much of it the first time, but after a couple more I sorta got to wondering. Looks to me like the hellion has been eyeing that shipping herd. Might not mean anything, but then again it might. Sort of a lonely trail to Sierra Blanca and the loading pens, with the Rio Grande and Mexico not far off. My hands are old fellers, like myself, and not as spry as they used to be and not as good in a ruckus. So I was wondering, Trev, if you could sorta give us an escort for part of the way, anyhow. Maybe I can get Sheriff Hart of Hudspeth to take over at your county line."

Slade and the sheriff exchanged glances. Serby nodded. The Ranger asked a few questions.

"As I understand, Mr. Cooley, your pasture where you are assembling the herd is also lonely, and not too far from the river?"

"That's right," said Cooley.

"And anybody grabbing off your herd from pasture would have a short and easy run to the river and Mexico."

"Guess that's right, too," Cooley admitted.

"You have a night guard posted over your cows?"

"Yep, two of the boys keep an eye on 'em."

"And if your suspicions are well founded, somebody will be keeping an eye on *them*," Slade said grimly.

"Do you have a couple of old horses trained to circle the herd without being guided?" he asked. "Most spreads do."

"Uh-huh, we got several," Cooley replied. He chuckled.

"We're all old-timers, down there, even the cayuses. Just what are you getting at, Mr. Slade?"

"Just this," the Ranger replied. "In my opinion there will not be a try for your shipping herd on the trail between here and Sierra Blanca. For the good and sufficient reason that, had you not come to the sheriff as you did, you would have had no herd to run to Sierra Blanca. Also, you would have very likely been short two hands. Your herd will be ready to roll day after tomorrow?"

"That's right," repeated Cooley, who was beginning to look decidedly worried.

Slade glanced at the sheriff. "Trevis," he said, "this may be the break we've been hoping for. It looks quite a bit that way to me. Would appear the hellions have never made a try at widelooping. Just the sort of thing they figure would catch us off guard, as the other two jobs did. Yes, this may be it. Mr. Cooley, I assume that herd represents a sizeable sum of money. Right?"

"It sure does, a hefty chunk—a lot more'n I'd care to lose— but I'm more worried about my boys than my cows."

"You won't lose the cows, or the boys, either, if you do just as I tell you and make no slips," Slade promised. "Now here's how we'll work it—an old trick, but under the circumstances I think it will be successful." He glanced at the door and the windows, making sure nobody was within hearing distance, lowered his voice and spoke earnestly for several moments. Cooley and the sheriff listened intently, the rancher tugging his mustache and nodding his head from time to time.

"Okay, Mr. Slade," he said when the Ranger paused. "I'll string right along with you; I figure you know your business."

"He does," the sheriff said, with emphasis.

"Just one thing," added Cooley, "I want to be along. After all, they're my cows you fellers will be taking a chance to look after."

"Glad to have you," Slade instantly acceded. Old Branch Cooley looked to be a salty proposition and a cool head. He would be an asset, not a liability.

20

THE FOLLOWING AFTERNOON, Sheriff Serby's three deputies rode north out of El Paso toward the New Mexico State Line. A report had been received—it was said—that there was trouble in that area between some sheep herders and some cowhands.

Slade and the sheriff ate dinner at Pablo's cantina. A little later Serby headed for home, and presumably, for bed. Not long afterward Slade, after a few words of explanation to Carmen, repaired to his hotel room.

As it happened, however, neither went to bed. Shortly before midnight, Sheriff Serby left his dwelling, saddled his horse and rode north. Half an hour later, Slade slipped from the hotel, got the rig on Shadow and also headed north. On a rise outside of town he halted the big black and for some minutes studied his back trail. Finally convinced he was not wearing a tail, he turned south by east on the Valley Trail, riding warily, watching the growth on either side. He had covered but a little more than a mile when a horseman rode from the brush, huge, distorted in the starlight. Slade waved his hand. The sheriff waved back. Slade reined in beside him and again studied the back trail, which stretched lonely and deserted, and his confidence was renewed that he had not been followed. He and the sheriff rode on down the valley at a fast pace, heading for old Branch Cooley's ranchhouse, which the deputies, who had turned back south with the coming of darkness, were fast approaching.

"Darned if I don't believe it's going to work," Serby observed.

"Beginning to look a little that way," Slade conceded. "I'm sure nobody spotted us leaving town. With a little good luck we may be able to clean up this mess once and for all. I hope so, for it's beginning to get a bit monotonous."

Serby grunted agreement, and they rode on. It was still dark when they reached the Flying Diamond casa, where they received a warm welcome from Cooley.

All day they remained at the ranchhouse without venturing out, against the possibility of prying eyes, although Slade did not think they had anything to worry about. In the course of the day, the last cows were combed out for the shipping herd, which was held in close herd on the banks of a little stream that meandered down from a spring in the hills.

The location was several miles northwest of the ranchhouse and close to where the chaparral growth, sprawling out from the base of the slopes for some distance, encroached on the valley floor.

The cows, heavily fleshed, fed full on the lush grass, showed no desire to drift.

At sunset, all but two of the hands rode in to the ranchhouse. A little later two headed for the herd, the nighthawks who would take over the chore of guarding the cattle through the dark hours. They rode slowly, taking their time as the shadows deepened. After a short conference with the two day guards—now it was almost full dark—all four rode into a nearby thicket, of which there were several scattered about in the neighborhood of the herd. There they busied themselves with certain rather curious preparations.

Once again all four horses approached the herd, which now was huddled, the cows one by one lying down to chew their cuds. Two horsemen rode back in the direction of the ranchhouse. Around and around the herd ambled two horses, with figures hunched wearily in the saddles, indistinct shadows in the starlight.

From time to time the horses would pause for a brief rest, then mosey on. The "riders" apparently allowed them to take their own course, in which there was nothing unusual. The seasoned cowhand could easily catch his forty winks in the hull, relying on his mount to handle the chore in the proper manner, which the trained cayuses would always do.

Meanwhile, six riders drifted along in the deeper shadow at the edge of the northern growth, their horses' irons making but a whisper of sound on the thick turf. Their objective was an arm of chaparral that thrust out from the main body of growth, where they would find ample concealment and at the same time see all that went on in the vicinity of the herd.

It was a nervous business, though, with no guarantee that at any moment they wouldn't be met by a burst of gunfire. Somewhere in the dense growth to the north, Slade was convinced, were murderous wideloopers who would show no mercy if they detected the posse making for the sanctuary of the belt of growth. They might even be holed up in the belt, waiting for the moon to rise and give them a better shooting light. El Halcon glanced apprehensively toward the eastern horizon, which was already brightening, turned his gaze ahead.

"Another five minutes and we'll make it," he said in low tones to his companions. "Here's hoping I haven't made a mistake. I don't think I have, though. We've been pretty well hidden from the slopes, and their attention, if they're there, will be centered on the herd."

The others nodded nervously and peered ahead. Now the belt of thicket was to be seen. Dark and silent it lay before them, the brush bristling up stiffly, for not a breath of wind stirred.

Closer and closer, with that blocky shadow seeming to exude a nameless threat. To the Ranger's vivid imagination, it took unto itself the shape of a vast predatory prehistoric beast, waiting, waiting. He glanced at his companions. They sat stiffly erect in their saddles, evincing uncomfortable nervous tension. He breathed relief as they reached the outer straggle of the growth, although he knew they were not yet wholly in the clear. It would be impossible to force their way into the brush without making a little noise, which would reach possible listening ears. He motioned to his companions to dismount.

Now the eastern sky was glowing with moonrise, but in another moment the black shadow of the growth swallowed the posse.

Leading their mounts, they edged along toward the far terminus of the brush, pausing from time to time to peer and listen.

From the blackness ahead came the mutter of a voice; the posse tensed.

But it was a reassuring mutter. Another moment and two cowhands stole forward to join them.

"Looks good," one muttered. "We ain't spotted a thing. Everything plumb quiet. If the hellions are there, I figure they don't suspect a mite."

"I hope not," Slade breathed reply. "If they really mean to make a try for the herd, we shouldn't have long to wait. They'll need time to get the cows to the river and across, where somebody will be waiting to receive them. They'll want them to be well on their way into Mexico before daylight."

However, the wait proved longer than he expected, filled as it was with nerve-racking suspense. Slowly an hour passed, and nothing happened. The two horses continued to amble around and around the herd, pausing for a few minutes at times then moseying on. The "riders" lurched and swayed, simulating weariness, seemingly hardly able to sit the hulls, lounging in the fashion of tired men in the dead hours of the night.

Slade began to wonder if the wideloopers had caught on and faded away into the darkness; he began to grow acutely uneasy. Looked like perhaps his carefully thought out plan had miscarried. It was an old trick, although it had worked for him before. He was heartened by the belief that the outlaws had reasoned nobody would suspect their design on the herd. But the slow minutes dragged past, and nothing happened.

The burst of gunfire was so sudden and so unexpected the posse jumped eight feet in the air—a foot to each man. The two "riders" jerked and lurched as bullets hammered them. The startled horses gave a convulsive bound. One "rider" toppled to the ground. The other slammed forward as if gripping the horn. The horses promptly bolted.

"Take over, Trevis," Slade whispered. "We're law enforcement officers and must give them a chance to surrender."

From the brush streamed six horsemen, heading for the alarmed herd. Sheriff Serby's voice rang out as the posse surged forward—

"Elevate! In the name of the law!"

There followed an instant of wild confusion as the raiders jerked their mounts to a rearing halt; metal gleamed.

"Let them have it!" Slade roared, and shot with both hands.

Two saddles were emptied by that first thundering volley. But the wideloopers, caught utterly by surprise, nevertheless fought back with vicious courage. Lances of fire split the moon-filtered darkness. The wan light distorted objects. The plunging horses rendered their riders elusive targets as they sidled their mounts back toward the growth and answered the posse shot for shot.

On Slade's left a deputy cursed shrilly. Another gave a yelp of pain. A slug grazed his own ribs, hurling him almost off balance with the shock. He reeled, recovered, fired as fast as he could pull trigger, counting his shots. A third raider fell.

A voice shouted a command. The outlaws whirled their horses, streaked for the brush. One, slightly in front, sat his mount with soldierly erectness, broad shoulders squared. Slade lined sights, but at that moment a deputy stumbled in front of him and he was forced to hold his fire. Before he could again get his Colt in line, the three had crashed into the brush and out of sight.

Reloading as he ran, Slade dashed to where he had left Shadow, flung himself into the saddle and raced in pursuit, the cursing posse streaming behind him.

But when they reached the dense and thorny growth they found themselves helpless to proceed. There was a way up the slope but in the black darkness they were unable to locate it. Finally, thoroughly disgusted, Slade called a halt.

"No use," he said. "They're gone. They know the way out, and we don't. Let's go back and see what we bagged."

"The murderin' snake-blooded skunks!" raved the sheriff. "If it had been two of the boys backing those nighthawk horses instead of overalls stuffed with straw, they'd been dead as Hector's pup. The blankety-blank sidewinders! Well, we busted up their little rustlin' scheme and did for some of 'em, anyhow."

"But, as usual, the one we wanted most got in the clear," Slade replied bitterly. "I'm beginning to think the hellion has a charmed life; the bullet doesn't seem to be run that can touch him."

"He'll get his before all is finished," growled Serby.

Slade's first concern was for the wounded deputies. He was thankful to find their hurts not serious, a bullet-sliced arm and a gashed thigh. Some salve and pads and bandages quickly took care of the injuries. There was a trickle of blood from his own grazed ribs, but he paid it no mind.

"We had the advantage, being on foot," he observed. "The back of a plunging horse isn't a very good shooting stance."

By the uncertain light, they gave the three bodies a once-over. Hard-looking characters, but nothing outstanding about them. Their pockets revealed nothing of significance save plenty of money.

The two nighthawk horses had not run far and were quickly rounded up. The bewildered cows had quieted.

"Lucky they weren't real old mossy-back longhorns," Slade remarked. "They would have scattered all over the section. Another advantage of improved stock; don't stampede so easily. Well, Trevis, guess we might as well load the carcasses and head for town. We all had a good sleep today, so there's no sense in hanging around."

The widelooper's horses had not followed the three that escaped and were caught without difficulty. Their brands were meaningless Mexican skillet-of-snakes burns, as Slade expected they would be.

They said goodbye to old Cooley and his hands, the rancher expressing his heartfelt thanks for what they had done for him, and headed for town with their grisly cargo.

Progress was slow, and it was past noon when they arrived in El Paso. After caring for the horses and disposing of the bodies, the sheriff and the deputies tumbled into bed. Slade repaired to Pablo's cantina where, as he expected, he found Carmen awaiting him.

"Yes, I did manage to get a couple of hours of sleep," she admitted. "But that was all, and I can sure stand a little more. Imagine you can, too. First, though, you're going to have something to eat. You must be starved."

21

SEVERAL HOURS LATER, after a good rest, Slade consulted with the sheriff.

"Well, anyhow we took that trick, even though we didn't rake in the whole pot as we hoped to," he remarked.

"Uh-huh, and we're sure whittling 'em down," said Serby.

"Yes, we are," Slade agreed thoughtfully. "I'm of the opinion that Parker, Regan and the one who got away with them are all that's left. What's bothering me more than anything else right now is the fear they will pull out. For we still have nothing on either of them. Being convinced of something in your own mind is one thing. Proving it to the satisfaction of twelve gentlemen in a jury box is quite another matter."

"And you think they might really trail their twine?"

"Not beyond the realm of possibility," Slade replied. "Things haven't been breaking well for them of late, save the train robbery, and they may well be getting quite nervous and figure that to stick around will be playing their luck too strong. Somehow, though, I'm getting a notion about something, and I may try playing a hunch. Can't see how it would do any harm, and it might be good."

The sheriff looked expectant, but Slade smilingly shook his head.

"Won't talk about it just yet," he said. "Haven't completely made up my mind. I'll tell you of it later."

"One of your loco lone-wolf schemes, I'll bet a hatful of pesos," the sheriff grumbled. "Oh, well, there's no stopping you when you've made up your mind to something."

All the following day Slade pondered the matter he had obliquely mentioned to Sheriff Serby. He frankly admitted it was a hunch, nothing more. A hunch without real foundation, hanging in the air. But so far as he could ascertain, he had nothing concrete to go on. And more and more he was convinced that Parker and Regan planned to pull out. With their bunch decimated, and then some, things going wrong for them at every turn and El Halcon on their trail, they might well reason that the section had gotten just a mite too hot and would seek fresh pastures. And there was nothing he could do to stop them.

His deductions were corroborated when he visited Pablo Montez later in the day.

"Heard talk that *amigo* Regan plans to sell," said Pablo. "Feller told one of my boys the head bartender is going to take over, that Regan bought a place in Sanderson when he was over east and will move there. May be just talk, but that's how it goes."

Slade was firmly of the opinion that it was more than talk. Then and there he decided to put his hunch to the test in a last attempt to apprehend or get rid of the villainous and elusive pair.

As a matter of fact, for some days Slade had not been able to get the old cabin in the clearing out of his mind. It didn't seem logical that the outlaws would visit the place again or put it to use, now its existence and location were known, but the hellions seemed to always shy away from the logical. They might gather there again to conduct one last foray, or for some obscure reason.

The more he thought about it, the more reasonable it became. Perhaps he was just talking himself into what he wished to believe, but the feeling persisted. It was almost as if something was calling him to the cabin. Later he was to wonder if such thought transference were not possible, ridiculous though such an assumption seemed.

The upshot of it all was that he could not banish the blasted place from his thoughts. Oh, well, he had nothing else to do, so why not?

Once again the dark hours before the dawn found him riding the old Indian track. He rode watchful and alert, although he really had little fear of meeting anybody on the trail. And now, as he pondered the matter under the calm stars, the whole business appeared silly. Following hunches had often proved wise, but there was a limit to how ridiculous one could get.

"Anyhow, it's a nice night for a ride, and sunrise is beautiful in these woods," he told Shadow. "You wanted to stretch your legs, and I hankered to go places, so we both got our wishes. So stop your snorting and take it easy."

Shadow let go a particularly large and derisive one as his opinion of the whole loco affair, pricked his ears and ambled on.

The eastern sky was rose and gold with the dawn long before

Slade reached the point where he would turn his mount into the brush. Birds were singing, and soon the level beams of the rising sun glinted on the leaves. He rode slowly, and the morning was well along when he secreted his mount in the chaparral and on foot made his way to the edge of the growth that flanked the clearing. Peering through the final screen, he surveyed the cabin for a long time, seeking an indication of possible occupancy.

To all appearances the old shack was deserted. No smoke rose from the mud-and-stick chimney. The windows remained unshadowed. There were no horses tethered under the lean-to. Began to look like his hunch was strictly out of order. He waited a while longer, still with no results. Finally he concluded he'd just embarked on a wild goose, or wild cabin, chase. Might as well head back to town.

First, however, he decided to have a look inside the building and see if he could discover any evidence of the outlaws' return after the fight in the cabin and the recovery of the stolen bank money. He left his place of concealment, sauntered to the door and pushed it open.

And looked squarely into the muzzle of a gun.

"Up!" said a voice behind the gun. "Get 'em up!"

Slade "got 'em up"—there was nothing else to do. He was caught settin'! Hands shoulder high, he gazed at the bristly-bearded, hard-featured individual whose gleaming black eyes peered over the gun barrel. Seething with anger, directed at himself, he obeyed the order when the fellow told him to turn around.

A cautious hand reached out, plucked the big Colts from their sheaths. His captor backed farther into the cabin.

"All right, turn around and walk in," he ordered. "Careful now, don't make any funny moves; I got a itchy trigger finger."

Without speaking, Slade entered the cabin, the outlaw backing away, careful to keep out of arm's reach. Without turning his head, he tossed Slade's guns onto one of the bunks. Then he stood for a moment, surveying the Ranger with his hot eyes.

"So!" he gloated. "The great El Halcon! Purty smart, eh? But not quite smart enough. The boss figured you'd come snoopin' around here again, sooner or later. Been waiting for you to show up."

Still Slade said nothing. There was really nothing to say. He had blundered into a trap with all the finesse of a gawky yearling. Something calling to him from the cabin? Began to look like there really had been. And he had answered the call with bells on!

"Boss will be here after a while," his captor resumed. "He'll have a few things to say to you—first. Reckon you won't be bothering us any more after today."

He eyed his captive speculatively a moment, then drew a chair to the broad and heavy table, his gaze never leaving Slade, and sat down. He gestured with his gun barrel to another chair on the far side of the table.

"Sit down there, with your hands up," he directed. "Now put your hands on the table and inch your chair up. Right! Keep your hands on top of the table."

Slade obeyed, his hands resting on the table top, fingers widespread. What the outlaw did not notice was that his thumbs were hooked *under* the table top. And those thumbs were strong as woven steel.

For a long moment the outlaw regarded him with his glittering eyes. The muzzle of his gun pointed straight at Slade's breast, and the gun was at full cock. He was alert, watchful, was taking no chances with his prisoner. The table was too wide to be reached across, even were El Halcon given the chance to do so, which was very unlikely. Slade decided to talk a little, ask a question or two. Might be possible to divert the fellow's attention for the split second he needed to go into action. Already his keen mind had formulated a plan that might work, if he could just get the chance to put it into effect.

"Who figured this scheme, Parker or Regan?" he asked.

The other grinned, showing yellow snags of teeth, his lips writhing back like the lethal grimace of a fanging rattlesnake.

"Parker's the big boss, as I guess you know," he replied. "He's the smart one. Uh-huh, plumb smart," he added pridefully. "You ain't bad yourself," he added with grudging respect. "You tangled our twine for us proper a few times, but I allus knew Big Bruce would drop a loop on you sooner or later. He did."

Slade was inclined to agree with him; there was an unpleasant modicum of truth in what he said. And if he, Slade, didn't manage to do something about it before Parker arrived on the scene, it would be curtains for him; he suffered no illusions as to that. He tried another question, his cold eyes boring into the outlaw's in hope of distracting the other's attention for an instant. The fellow shifted his gaze a little under that hard stare, but otherwise did not appear to be affected.

"Parker a Texan?" Slade asked. The fellow moved his head a little from side to side.

"Nope, he's from Oklahoma," he replied. " 'Leastwise that's where I knew him first."

Slade nodded. "Know him quite a while?" he asked.

"About a year," the other replied.

"Why did he come here?"

The fellow shrugged. "Things were getting a mite hot up there. He heard about this section and figured there'd oughta be some good pickin's here. There was." He glowered. "That is, till you came along and tried to horn in. Well you tried that little game once too often."

A silence followed. Slade still sat in the same position, his thumbs hooked under the table top. The outlaw still kept his cocked gun trained on the Ranger's breast. Slade noted that from time to time his eyes glinted sideways toward the open door. He was expecting somebody, all right. And time might be getting very short. He'd have to act quickly, no matter how desperate a chance he'd have to take. Once let Parker and perhaps Regan show up, and he'd have no chance at all. He racked his brains for a solution to the problem. The plan had crystallized in his mind, but it was absolutely necessary to distract the fellow's attention for a split second if it were to be successful.

Suddenly he jerked his head up, staring at the window across the room, his eyes widening, mouth dropping open as if in utter amazement.

Instinctively the outlaw turned his head. The gun muzzle wavered the merest trifle. With all his strength, Slade jerked and shoved. Over went the table. The gun blazed. The slug fanned Slade's face. Then table, chair and outlaw crashed to the floor together.

Slade went over the upturned table in a streaking dive. The gun boomed again, but Slade's iron grip was on the outlaw's wrist, and the bullet thudded into the ceiling. Up and back he bent the other's arm, while the fellow frantically tried to bring the muzzle to bear. His free hand shot out, closed on Slade's throat in a throttling grip. Over and over they rolled. The chair went to kindling wood. The table slithered across the floor. Slade slashed blows at the other's face, but he ducked his head and took the blows on the top of his bristly skull, where they apparently had no effect. And ever his strangling grip on the Ranger's throat tightened.

Slade's breath was shut off. His chest labored. Red flashes stormed before his eyes. The outlaw was a big man, and he seemed to be made of steel wires. He had managed to get the gun cocked again and was striving desperately to bring it to bear. His wrist was coming down a little as El Halcon's strength ebbed for lack of air.

With all his might, Slade jerked the gunhand down, throwing himself sideways in the same flash of movement.

The gun exploded. Blood gushed over Slade's hand. The outlaw gave a strangled cry. His body jerked, relaxed and ceased to move. He had obligingly shot himself through the neck.

22

REELING, STAGGERING, GULPING air into his tortured lungs, Slade floundered erect, leaned with one hand against the wall and gazed down at his dead foe. The hellion had put up a darn good fight but, to paraphrase his own remark, not quite good enough.

For several minutes Slade leaned against the wall, until his chest ceased pounding, his nerves steadied. Then he retrieved his guns and holstered them. Glancing about the cabin littered with wrecked furniture, he pondered what should be his next move. Should he remain in the cabin until Parker, and possibly somebody else, put in an appearance? Very quickly he resolved not to do so. After his recent experience in the shack he had developed a love of life in the open. Stay inside and he might get trapped again.

From a cunningly hidden secret pocket in his broad leather belt he took something that gleamed in the sunlight—a silver star set on a silver circle, the feared and honored badge of the Texas Rangers. The time for concealment was over.

He pinned the badge to his shirt front, left the cabin and closed the door. Quickly he found a place in the growth from where he could see all sides of the clearing and settled down to wait.

It proved to be a long and tedious wait. The sun crossed the zenith, slanted down the western sky, and Slade began to wonder just what the dead outlaw had meant when he said "after a while." Slade had interpreted the remark to mean that Parker would show up shortly, which was substantiated by his frequent glances toward the door.

The minutes dragged past. Suddenly Slade lifted his head. To his keen ears had come a sound, the sound of horses' hoofs on the trail beyond the growth. Another moment and two men rode into the clearing—Bruce Parker and Clay Regan—and headed for the cabin.

Slade stepped from the growth, his face set, his eyes coldly gray as the waters of a glacier lake. His voice rang out, edged with steel—

"In the name of the State of Texas! You are under arrest."

For an instant Parker and Regan stared at the grim figure confronting them. Then, with a yell of rage, Parker went for the gun he wore in a shoulder holster under his black coat. The clearing jumped to the bellow of reports.

Once again the man on the ground had the advantage. Seconds later, Walt Slade, one hand dripping blood, one boot top shredded, lowered his smoking Colts and gazed at the two forms sprawled on the ground. Holstering one gun, he moved forward, alert and watchful, then he holstered the other.

Regan was dead, shot squarely between the eyes. Parker, with two bullets through his chest, was going fast. He glared up at Slade. His dying gaze centered on the gleaming silver star.

"A Ranger!" he gurgled through the blood welling in his throat. "El Halcon a—Texas—Ranger! They—told—me not to go—to—Texas—that the Rangers would—get—me. They—did!"

His chest arched, fell in; his eyes closed, and he was dead.

Mechanically, Slade caught the two horses, flipped out the bits and led them to the lean-to and filled their feed boxes. Then he browsed around in the growth until he located the third outlaw's horse, knee-haltered in another little clearing where grass grew. He found the rig concealed beneath some sacks in the lean-to. After which he retrieved Shadow and fed him.

While the horses ate, he entered the cabin, found a boiler of coffee, still slightly warm. He kindled a fire, heated it up a bit and drank several cups. Then, feeling somewhat better, he enjoyed a cigarette.

His next chore was to laboriously rope the bodies to the saddles. With a final glance around at the clearing of death, he set out on the long ride to town.

When Walt Slade rode through the streets of El Paso, the three burdened horses trailing behind, men stared but did not speak, for the look of his face forbade questions. A crowd was following close as he drew rein in front of the sheriff's office and dismounted.

"Keep a watch on those critters, will you, please?" he requested of the crowd, gesturing toward the led horses.

Sheriff Serby was seated in his swivel chair, his boots on his desk. The boots came to the floor with a bang.

"Now what?" he demanded.

Slade slumped wearily into a chair. "Outside you'll find a few souvenirs, and I guess this is about all," he replied.

The sheriff hurried outside. A few minutes later he came pounding back into the office.

"You got them both!" he exploded. "What—what—how—"

Slade told him, briefly, for he was very tired. Serby exclaimed in amazement, shook his head and swore.

"You're the limit!" he declared. "Yes, the plumb limit. 'About all,' you said? Well, I reckon it's enough!"

"Now what?" he added.

"Now," Slade answered, "if you'll take over, I'll stable my horse and then amble down to Pablo's place. I crave something to eat and a chance to look at somebody nice. I'll see you after a while. I'll have to head back to the Post soon, to see what Captain Jim has lined up for me."

Two days later Carmen, his kiss still warm on her lips, watched him ride away, tall and graceful atop his tall black horse, to where duty called and danger and new adventure waited. She smiled, a little tremulously.

"Uncle Pablo," she said, "he's wonderful and I'm crazy about him, but as I told you once before, I don't think I could take it for a lifetime."